# IOTA CYCLE

Published by Silverthought Press
www.silverthought.com

ISBN: 0-9774110-4-4

# IOTA CYCLE

## Russell Lutz

[silverthought]
Philadelphia ]{ New York

*for my parents*

*"It is not our part here to take thought only for a season, or for a few lives of Men, or for a passing age of the world."*
*--J. R. R. Tolkien*

# Contents

# THE BURKE FAMILY

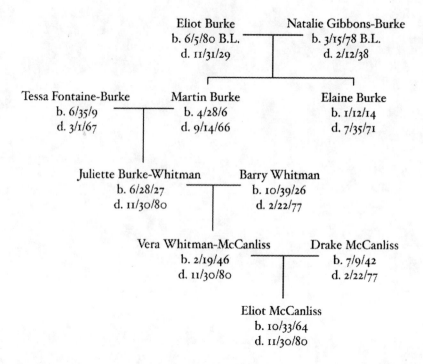

Eliot Burke
b. 6/5/80 B.L.
d. 11/31/29

Natalie Gibbons-Burke
b. 3/15/78 B.L.
d. 2/12/38

Tessa Fontaine-Burke
b. 6/35/9
d. 3/1/67

Martin Burke
b. 4/28/6
d. 9/14/66

Elaine Burke
b. 1/12/14
d. 7/35/71

Juliette Burke-Whitman
b. 6/28/27
d. 11/30/80

Barry Whitman
b. 10/39/26
d. 2/22/77

Vera Whitman-McCanliss
b. 2/19/46
d. 11/30/80

Drake McCanliss
b. 7/9/42
d. 2/22/77

Eliot McCanliss
b. 10/33/64
d. 11/30/80

# PROLOGUE

Earth

April 18, 80
*(February 25, 2363)*


The Prime Minister leaned forward across her desk, a heavy oak and brass affair, a gift from one of the American Senators, either Texas or Mississippi Valley, she couldn't remember which. The Senator she addressed across this desk was the Gentleman from Hunan.

"You don't have the votes in the chamber, you don't have the will of the people to swing those votes, you don't have the money to buy those votes, and you don't have my support to bolster the significant inadequacies of your effort. Is that clear enough for you? I suggest you let the bill die painlessly in committee."

Senator Liu stood.

"I thank you for your time, Ms. Prime Minister."

He stalked out the door. Fox, Prime Minister Guaraldi's adjutant, came into the office a moment later, sporting a knowing grin. Guaraldi shook her head.

"Why do I let them get to me?"

"Because you let them into the room, for one thing," Fox said.

"You're the one who lets them into the room, Fox."

"Of course, Prime Minister. And the next one I'm

letting in is Minister Ashburne."

"Ashburne? Something happening outsystem that I don't know about?"

"I wouldn't know, sir."

"You would know."

"That's true. But in this case, I don't."

"Send him in."

Fox slid out and Ashburne stepped in. Felix Ashburne was a rarity in government: a bona fide academic. The now customary process of colonizing the systems of distant stars still provided many more scientific obstacles than political ones, and Ashburne was the right man to overcome them. Despite this—or perhaps because of it—he was still humbled by the room; he came in apologetically.

"Ms. Prime Minister?"

"Come in, Felix." Guaraldi stood to put Ashburne at ease. "Come in. It's been a while." She gestured to one of the chairs and Ashburne sat, thankful.

"It's been two months, ma'am."

"Something up?"

"Yes, ma'am. There's a problem with Iota Horologii. We lost contact three days ago." Ashburne indicated the voice input on the desk and asked, "May I?"

"Certainly."

Ashburne spoke in what was now considered computer-voice, a mellow yet distinct intonation that computers were designed to listen for so they wouldn't respond to random conversation. "Iota Horologii system map. Desk size." A hologram of the six-planet system blossomed over the desk.

"Lost... Wait a minute. Iota was one of the earlier colonies?" Guaraldi asked.

"The third, Prime Minister. *Hermione* left Earth 181 years ago, and the system has been thriving for 105 years."

"And we've lost contact?"

"Yes, ma'am."

"How is that possible?"

"Well, ma'am, we're convinced the problem is at their end. Exhaustive checks on our local beam assembly have shown it's functioning perfectly. Of course, there's the unlikely possibility that a highly dense object, a black hole or a brown dwarf, passed through the beam and broke it, but there's no indication of that in any of our stellar surveys. Anything less dense would have no impact on the neutrinos that make up—"

"Felix, why don't we focus on likely possibilities? Did they ever give an indication that they were having trouble with their assembly?"

"None, Prime Minister."

"Alright, lay out a best case/worst case scenario for me."

Ashburne swallowed. He was sweating. Guaraldi smiled, trying to help him calm down a little.

"The best case scenario is that their beam assembly broke down and they fixed it. They should be rebuilding their beam right now. If so, we'll know about it in fifty-six years, when the new beam reaches our assembly and we can regain contact."

"Fifty-six years... That's the *best* case scenario?"

"Yes, ma'am. It will take that long for the beam to be rebuilt."

"I don't know if I want to hear the worst case." Ashburne didn't take that well. He was visibly agitated. "I'm sorry," said Guaraldi. "Just a joke. Please, go on."

"Of course. The worst case scenario is... that Iota Horologii, despite everything we know to the contrary about stellar evolution, went supernova and destroyed the entire system in a few milliseconds."

Guaraldi involuntarily glanced at the glowing representation of Iota floating next to her husband's picture, irrationally worried it might explode even now.

Ashburne continued. "If that's what happened, we'll know about it in approximately thirty-two years."

"Thirty-two? Faster than light? How is that possible?"

"The *Telperion*. The resupply ship. Under the original Stellar Charter, before the Mackenzie Reform, each colony was to be resupplied with a new batch of colonists and upgraded technology. The hundredth anniversary of the formation of Iota was five years ago, and we sent *Telperion*. They still have an active beam with us. They'll see the

3

explosion when they're nearly halfway there, and they can tell us about it. If that's what happened."

"I see." Guaraldi stood to pace around the desk, walking absently through one of the slowly revolving planets. Ashburne jumped up, watching, waiting, worrying. Guaraldi said, "If I understand you correctly, we won't know anything at all for thirty-two years, at the very earliest."

"That's correct, Prime Minister."

"And there's nothing I can do to change that. Nothing I can do to rectify the situation. Nothing I can do... at all."

"Also correct, ma'am."

"You rushed into my office just to give me this news personally."

"Yes." Ashburne's voice trembled.

Guaraldi stopped next to her Minister for Extrasolar Affairs and put an arm around his shoulders. "I have never worked with a person who understood my job less than you, Felix."

"I... I..."

"Don't ever change."

"Thank you, ma'am." Ashburne scurried out. Fox returned instantly, but Guaraldi gave him an uncharacteristic wave, and the adjutant left her alone for the time being.

Guaraldi stood silently, looking at the colorful, picture-book vision of a planetary system that may or may not have been completely destroyed.

# EQUINOX

en route to Iota Horologii

September 19, 3 B.L.
*(April 23, 2255)*

The alarm in the stateroom was designed to wake Lois slowly. Soft music and gentle sounds of nature came from the speakers in the walls of the room at 7:00, at first only just audible. Slowly, ever so slowly, the volume increased, drawing Lois out of her slumber like a shy girl being coaxed to the dance floor. It was timed perfectly to match Lois's sleep cycle, the ramping sounds enticing her out of REM sleep, toward wakefulness. By 7:30, when the alarm would be at peak volume, Lois would open her eyes, completely rested and ready to start the day.

At 7:23, a buzzer went off, jolting Lois awake. She shut off the alarm and answered the call.

"What?"

"You up yet?" he asked over the intercom.

"Every day? Do you have to do this every day?"

"Sorry." A click as he shut off the intercom. Lois got out of bed.

⋄

It was ten of eight when Lois entered the bridge.

"What do you think the task—" Clark started immediately. Lois held up a hand.

"I'm not here. I have ten minutes."

Clark went into a predictable sulk. Lois walked the length of the bridge in ten steps, ignoring him. The room was roughly cylindrical, walls of metal and plastic, dominated by the command console in the center. It was so familiar it barely registered on her anymore. She stopped at the observation window, a plate of thick plexiglas that made up the rear quarter of the room's floor. Past the hazy corona of the ship's engine exhaust, she saw Iota glowing more brightly than any other star. Each day she tried to convince herself that the star *looked* closer than the day before... but she couldn't. Her vision was just not that good.

Lois felt Clark's eyes on her back. He wouldn't be glaring exactly; he would be frustrated, intent, like a puppy dog waiting to see if he'd get a treat or a smack on the nose. She knew that if she turned around right now he would instantly be engrossed in some minor detail on the main console. She smiled to herself, then forced the smile to disappear. She turned around.

Clark was running a finger down one of the view screens, mouthing as he counted. Lois walked around behind him, putting her hands on his shoulders, subconsciously massaging him.

"What are you looking at?"

"Just counting the recent flares on Iota."

"Really?"

"Could be important for colonies on the inner planets."

"I see."

Clark kept counting, and Lois watched, suppressing an urge to shout out something like "Twenty-seven!"

"Lois?"

"Yes?"

"You really want to screw up my counting, don't you?"

Lois laughed, and Clark laughed with her. He stood from the main console chair and gave her a kiss and a hug.

"You know me too well," she said.

"And you know me. So let's do the task!"

"Fine!"

Clark was in charge during the night shift, while Lois slept. Lois would take the bridge after Clark went to bed at 4 p.m. For the next eight hours, though, they shared control of the ship. Over the years, the routine had become second nature to them. Certain things Clark always did, like realignment of the beam to Earth. Other things were always Lois's responsibility, like determining the task for the day. She sat in the console chair and called up the task allocation program. She was about to press the icon labeled "Assign" when Clark put a hand on her arm.

"Wait."

"Why?"

"Guess what it'll be."

"Clark."

"C'mon. Guess."

"I can't. There are still more than a thousand tasks left. It's useless to guess."

"I think it'll be... The Question."

"It won't be The Question."

"Yes, it will. I can feel it. It'll be The Question. Do you know how you think we should answer?"

"It won't be. Trust me. It'll be a check of the cryo chambers or a scan of the hull plating. Something dull." Lois had never told Clark that she had programmed the computer to wait to give them The Question sometime during the final year of their voyage. She knew he'd see that as cheating, somehow.

"You're wrong. Mark my words," Clark said ominously, then added a self-satisfied nod. Lois pressed the icon. A line of text appeared on the screen. Lois smiled. Clark frowned.

"Name the planets?" Clark whined. "That'll take about three minutes."

"This is a very important responsibility. There are a hundred thousand people up there—" She pointed past the ceiling. "—who will be living and working in the Iota System for the rest of their lives, and we can shape their concept of their homes with these names."

"Yeah, like our designers spent more than three minutes

coming up with *our* names."

Lois put an arm around Clark's waist. "*I* think you're super!"

"Thanks." Lois could tell Clark was annoyed by the way he punched through the console menus to pull up a graphic of the Iota System on the wall screen that faced them. He unlatched the extra chair from the wall and rolled it over next to Lois. They sat and watched six planets slowly spin around Iota in an adulterated representation that was very much not to scale but made it possible to get a fair amount of detail onto the screen. Clark took the controls and started adjusting the view, making the system tilt and spin. First he set the view edge on, which made the relative orbits of the planets impossible to understand. Then top down, which offered views from above the planets' poles. That was worse.

"I'll do it," Lois said, and she swept the view to about fifteen degrees above the ecliptic. She jumped from the chair and moved to the screen.

When *Hermione* was designed, this display system and the identical one in the bridge at the top of the ship were supposed to provide vivid three-dimensional holographic imagery for the crew of two. The images the screens produced *were* vivid... and headache inducing. The 3-D function was deactivated on the other bridge after only two days in space. This one was modified soon after Lois and Clark relocated to the lower habitat for the second half of the journey to Iota Horologii. They had spent twenty-five years looking up through a ceiling panel at Iota as they accelerated toward her, and twenty-two years, so far, looking down at her as they decelerated towards Iotan insertion.

"We should start here," Lois said, indicating Iota's one gas giant, a teal and ochre planet, a little over twice as massive as Jupiter, and nearly one AU from Iota. A bonus that no one on Earth had expected during the planning stages of the mission: two of the moons orbiting the giant were large enough for terraforming. "This is the focus of the system. It should have a grand name... Gravitas. How's that?"

"Gravitas? So we're going to pick random nouns out of the dictionary? Why not call it Zymurgy?"

Lois pointed to the lonely, icy planet at the edge of the system. "That one looks more like a Zymurgy to me."

Clark shook his head at her.

"Maybe you're right," she said. "We should decide on the theme. What kinds of names should we give them?"

"Gods. Why break with tradition? Call the big one Hercules."

"Hercules wasn't a god. And we can't just ape the Solar System. We have to do something special, something that will fire the imagination of the colonists."

"I wish we'd gotten The Question."

"Be glad we didn't get the task of defining North."

Clark gave her an odd look. Lois came back to the controls and spun the entire system upside down.

"Maybe that should be the way we look at it."

"It's upside down."

"Why?"

Clark squinted at the planets, tilted his head, then changed the view back without comment.

"I guess that'll be an easy one when we get it," Lois said. Inspiration struck. "I know, let's name the planets after characters of fiction. Ishmael. Gilgamesh. Thisbe."

Clark started to laugh. "What's so funny?" she asked.

"Shylock! Sauron! Flagg!" He collapsed into giggles.

"It's not that funny."

Clark tried to stop laughing. "Yes, it is."

"You're impossible. I'm starting to think my answer to The Question will be 'Yes.'"

Clark stopped laughing. "What?"

"I can't have an opinion? I can't express an opinion?"

"No... It's just that... I thought—"

"You never said what *you* thought."

"I was waiting for you to..."

They looked at each other, the silence dragging on and on. Eventually, Clark left the bridge. Lois was left to stare at the unnamed planets and count solar flares alone.

☼

There were always fights. In forty-seven years, it was impossible not to fight many times. The worst one was in the third year. After that one, they didn't speak for ten days. It was an exception, though. Most disagreements lasted less than four hours, because they had gotten into a very odd habit: meeting for lunch. It was an odd habit because they never ate.

☼

At 11:57, Lois watched Clark slink back onto the bridge, roll his chair over to the console and sit next to her. He gave her a sad grin.

"Later?" he asked.

"Later."

She punched a button, and the Iota System reappeared on the screen, each planet now tagged with a name. Clark looked at the names, his sad grin becoming more amused.

"Odin... Thor... Loki... Who's Freya?"

"Goddess of Love and Beauty. I made the last planet Skadi, Goddess of Winter."

"Cute."

Lois caught Clark's eye. It wasn't really telepathy that passed between them, but something similar. Clark nodded and Lois erased the names.

"Okay," Clark said, "I was thinking of another way to go. Name the planets after Earth."

"Earth 1, Earth 2?"

"No." He started typing on the console. The lonely planet that had been briefly named Skadi became Maailma.

"What is that?" Lois asked.

"That's 'world' in Finnish." He typed again. The smallish planet closest to Iota became Ulimwengu. Clark beamed at Lois. "Swahili."

"Okay... Maybe."

Clark kept typing. The fourth planet, a grayish world that was a bit smaller than Venus, was now assigned the name Chikyuu.

"I get the idea," Lois said. "But it seems a little random. And all of these colonists are English speaking."

"They're not all Europeans and Americans."

"Most are." Clark added another name while Lois talked. "And they won't really respond emotionally to... Dahn Tu." Clark seemed disappointed.

"Oh... okay. I kind of wanted to give it a multi-cultural flair... Do you have any other ideas?"

Lois stared intently at the screen. "That one." She pointed at the third planet, a rocky world orbiting at 1.2 AU from Iota, big enough to provide near-Earth gravity. It had a wispy atmosphere of nitrogen and some other trace gasses. There was also a small amount of water frozen at the poles. It was more than enough to jumpstart the terraforming efforts there. "That has to be the focus. It's the best planet in the system."

"You think?" Clark was engaged now. He used the console to zoom in on this planet. "What's the rotational period?"

"Twenty-five hours and a few seconds."

"You're kidding? Axial tilt?"

"Seventeen degrees."

"This is perfect! This is the next Earth!"

"It does look pretty good to me. It's in the shadow of the gas giant for a few hours every two years, but..."

"Everyone is going to want to live there. It'll cause problems."

Lois didn't want to argue with Clark. He might have been right, but assignment to specific planets or moons wasn't up to the individual colonists themselves. A commission would divide them according to their talents and the challenges each planet would present. For example, even at this distance, the grayish fourth planet was showing signs that it might have life, which meant if a group did settle there it would have to be very small, and their mix would be heavy on scientists, mostly biologists. Populating the Iota System would require a hundred thousand choices. Lois was glad she and Clark wouldn't have to make them.

"Okay," Clark said, "so this third planet is like a utopia... Hey, how about Utopia?"

"It's a little presumptive."

"Shangri-La?"

"Valhalla?" Lois suggested.

"What is it with you and Scandinavians?"

"Are you really thinking of saying 'No'?" she asked.

Clark tensed up. Lois watched his fingers lift slightly from the console surface. "Do you really want to talk about this now?"

"We're not getting anywhere with the task. We might as well."

"Okay." Clark spun the chair to face Lois directly. She swiveled the command chair around, too. She was sitting up a little higher, so she leaned forward, elbows on knees, to bring them to the same level. They were only a few centimeters apart. "Here's my thinking. We've been on this ship for seventy-two years, and—"

"Forty-seven," she interrupted.

"Don't start."

"Start what?"

"With the time dilation crap. You know I don't buy it," Clark said, his voice rising.

"There's nothing to buy. We're in contact with Earth every day. The beam sends signals to Earth instantaneously. We *see* time dilation happening, in real time."

"It's an illusion." Clark's face lost its playful openness, replaced by pure truculence.

"How can you, I, the ship's clock, and every elementary particle you can break into pieces all be under the spell of an illusion?"

"This trip is taking seventy-five years."

"But to us, it's fifty."

"How long is a year?"

"What?"

"What's the definition of a year?"

"I see what you're doing," she said, trying to derail his argument before he got started. "It's not—"

"A year is the length of time that the Earth takes to go

around the Sun."

"Yes, but—"

"How many times has the Earth gone around the Sun while we've been gone?"

"Clark, you're—"

"Seventy-two. Seventy-two *years*."

"That's just semantics."

Clark pointed at the screen where the Earthlike planet was still rotating. "And spending all day trying to come up with valid, emotional, important names for these isn't semantics?"

"That's different."

Lois saw what was happening. Clark was working himself into a lather, and she couldn't really stop him. It was an old pattern with them.

"It's only different because you say it's different. Words can have value that even *you* don't see." Clark was on the edge of saying something more, but he stopped and walked off the bridge again. Lois got as far as the door before she stopped and went back to the console.

It her took an hour to find the logs for the day they had the big fight forty-four (or sixty-nine) years ago, but she found them. Their task that day was assigned, as always, randomly by the computer. They had to test *Hermione's* telescope on the Solar System. It was fitted with what was then the latest rectilinear zoom technology. Even at such a distance, the detail on the planets, particularly Mars, was staggering. Clark was convinced he could see Robinson Lake in the southern hemisphere. Lois thought he was deluding himself.

But what caused the blowup back then? Lois was sure that something about the day's task had set Clark off then—and now. It was more than simple anxiety about how they would answer The Question once *Hermione* arrived at Iota. At least, she thought it was.

Maybe she was overanalyzing. It was three years into the journey that they had the big fight... and it was now three years from completion that they were having this one. There was a certain balance to it.

She gave up thinking about it and went to the
stateroom. Clark was lying on his side of the bed, staring at
the ceiling. Lois crawled up onto her side, head tilted to
look at him. She smiled at the familiar features: his sharp
nose with just a few freckles, his strong jaw, his dark, brown
eyes that matched his wavy hair. She had long since
accepted the fact that she was designed to be attracted to
him, as he was to her. She had wrestled with that for years,
but now she felt lucky that she hadn't had to endure a
chancy game of sexual hide-and-seek with an entire
population of men. Someone had put them together. It
wasn't perfect, that was certain. But there was a symmetry
to them that she couldn't imagine biology matching.

Without speaking, she sidled over to him. Nothing was
resolved, not time dilation, not The Question, and certainly
not the names of the planets in the Iota System. But this
was something they had that they didn't have to think too
much about. She kissed him, and it was only a second or
two before he started kissing back.

✿

They spooned quietly, Clark's face nuzzling her neck.
She thought he might be close to falling asleep, which was
fine. It was nearly four o'clock.

"I'm scared," he said.

"You are?"

"Do you ever wonder what it would be like to want to
have children?"

Lois stopped breathing.

"I do," he continued, his voice barely audible. "I don't
really wonder about children themselves. They programmed
us too well for that. But I wonder about the *urge*. I kind of
wish sometimes, just sometimes, that I knew what it was
like to have a parental instinct. So I think they didn't build
us perfectly."

Lois felt tears welling up.

"I get why we have to have The Question. We've been

in space, alone, for... for decades, and if we have to do that again... well, maybe they're right, and we might go a little... crazy. But if Iota checks out, if we can thaw out the colonists and help them build a new life, I want to keep all the memories of this trip. I don't want my memory wiped. I want to answer 'No' when they ask. And I guess the reason is that if they didn't make us perfect, then, if I forget all this, and you forget all this... I don't know if we'll still love each other."

Now Lois was crying. She tried not to sniff, but she had to. When she did, Clark pulled her a little closer before continuing.

"I don't want to go anywhere. I want to stay around Iota, with you. I want to keep being the person I am now, and I want you to, too."

He kissed her shoulder. She shook with a last little sob, then rolled over to look at Clark. He was almost asleep. She kissed him on the nose, and started to pull herself out of bed when she remembered something.

"Clark... Clark?"

"Hm?"

"The task. We never came up with names."

Only half awake, Clark mumbled, "...continents on Earth..."

She smoothed his hair and whispered, "Okay."

# LANDING

Europe

January 1, 1
*(May 4, 2258)*

The sky above Europe was a light tan color, a pale mirror of the dusty landscape. Without much of an atmosphere, there were no clouds to block the faint light of the stars, the ruddy glow of Asia, the harsh rays of Iota.

It started as a barely perceptible dot low in the morning sky. An observer on the plateau would have had difficulty determining what the thing was. It didn't appear to be a meteor, because even in the thin methane air, a meteor would have been burning by now.

As the dot grew larger, details appeared.

The lander design—officially known as a Boeing 4344—had been nicknamed a "raven" because of its black-metal construction, its forward-pointed cockpit and its swept-back wings. *Hermione* had carried two ravens strapped to the outside of her hull across fifty-three light years of space to Iota Horologii.

As the first captain of this raven, Eliot Burke had the honor of naming her. He had dubbed her *Icarus*.

✿

Just before waking from his long sleep, Eliot had

dreamed of bison. In the irrefutable inner logic of the dream, he found it quite normal that he was driving a herd of bison across the hills of Wyoming. Of course, Eliot had never been to Wyoming, and had never ridden a horse, and hadn't come within five hundred kilometers of a bison in his life. He'd always lived in cities—Tucson, Orlando, Hong Kong. One of the reasons he relished the opportunity to travel to a new solar system was the chance to live in a real place, a place with human dimensions, where you know your neighbors and you can raise a family, where you are close to the land.

The insistent thud of hooves on fertile ground slowly transformed to the persistent beat of Eliot's own heartbeat in his ears. He was immersed in half-frozen gel, lying on his back in a coffin-like freezing chamber. He waited patiently for someone to open his bed and pull him out of the artificial womb he'd been living in for more than seven decades.

Finally a seal broke and Eliot heard a far-away whistle of air slicing into his little space. The lid tipped up and strong arms dipped into the blue slush to pull Eliot's head up into warm air. They removed his face mask and allowed him three unsteady breaths before asking:

"What's your name?"

The man helping Eliot into a seated position had a dark complexion and frizzy black hair. He looked at Eliot closely, as if searching for some deep truth.

"Eliot Burke."

The man turned his head and yelled across the freezing bay: "Eliot Burke!"

The focus of Eliot's eyes grew sharper, and he saw fifty people milling about the room, some dressed in casual clothes, others draped in blankets, recently awakened. All of them looked at Eliot expectantly. He felt a shiver of nervousness. He was only one of a hundred thousand colonists. Why did they care so much about him? And why didn't they already know his name? Something was wrong.

He recognized the man at the far side of the bay: Clark, one of *Hermione*'s android pilots. He typed Eliot's name into a screen on the wall.

"Well?" the strong man asked.

"I... I think he's a 'maybe'," Clark said.

✧

The working theory was that some unseen solar flare from a passing star had scrambled the index files for the colonists. Since the system containing all their personal information was in the freezing bays, away from the heavily shielded main *Hermione* computer, that was a plausible explanation. The androids would never have known. The colonists were protected from the flare by the freezing gel; the computer wasn't.

The mission parameters, carefully constructed by the Ministry of Extrasolar Affairs nearly a century ago, laid out a specific sequence in which the colonists would be awakened. Among the first were the construction specialists who would build the initial pressurized structures on the surface of Europe. Those with skills in low-oxygen botany were next; they were needed to start up a rudimentary agriculture on the planet. Communications specialists would calibrate the beam assembly in its polar orbit of the star for the link to Earth. Doctors would care for the sick. Cooks would prepare food. A dozen different skill sets were required in the early stages of an extra-solar colony.

But first, they needed a pilot.

✧

Another pocket of turbulence rocked *Icarus*. The pilot and navigator kept silent while the passengers gave a collective yelp of fear.

"You'd think at 0.02 atmospheres of pressure there wouldn't be this much..." John, the navigator, didn't finish the thought.

"You'd think," Eliot answered. His hands were cramping

on the flight yoke. He didn't dare raise a hand to wipe the sweat from his face. He watched the altimeter wind down. With a largely unmapped countryside below them, he wasn't sure how much value the device provided. It couldn't warn him about every little mountain that might lie in their path. That's what John was for, after all. His eagle eyes continued to scan the horizon ahead.

Eighteen other colonists sat belted into the seats behind the cockpit of the raven. Behind them, in the broad belly of the ship, lay the construction materials for a temporary shelter. Eliot was flying them toward one of the equipment drops that *Hermione* had sent to the surface during the past several weeks. In a reinforced orbital container lying on the European surface was everything needed to start a colony on an Earth-like planet: construction materials, radiation-hardened electronic equipment, water, food, clothing. The supplies in the back of the raven were a backup, in case they landed too far afield. When *Icarus* landed, they were going to put down roots, one way or another.

Eliot had been a pilot back on Earth—in his spare time. It was little more than a hobby for him. There were two women and one man on *Hermione* who had logged several hundred hours of flight time in ravens. Unfortunately, the one pilot who had been thawed out was experiencing severe hibernation sickness, and the other two pilots hadn't been found yet.

The colonization was weeks behind schedule. Europe was approaching conjunction with Asia, and the android pilots didn't think it was wise to do drops from *Hermione* during such a close pass to the gas giant. The landing had to be now. Otherwise, they would have to wait for fifty days or so for Asia to retreat to a safe distance.

The population of conscious people on the ship had started taxing *Hermione*'s design. There weren't places for all of them to eat, sleep, bathe. They needed to get the colony started as soon as possible.

When asked, Eliot agreed to pilot the first landing to the surface of Europe.

✧

The turbulence didn't really bother him. The raven was basically a flying tank. It was their speed that had him very concerned. He hadn't understood fully until now the importance of drag in flying a fixed-wing aircraft. Eliot had extended *Icarus*'s wings to their limit; they provided the raven with enough lift to keep her from slamming into the ground like a stone. He was still going entirely too fast from his orbital insertion to make a safe landing. Their proposed site for the initial camp was coming up, and Eliot wasn't sure what to do. He thought for half a second of calling back up to *Hermione* and asking them to put Elaine Karpaski—the sick raven pilot—on the line to talk him down. Unfortunately, by the time they brought her to the bridge, *Icarus* would already have crashed.

"There's the plateau," John said.

On the horizon, Eliot saw their landing site. It was a fairly level parcel of land next to a dry ocean bed. They were flying over the ancient ocean now, but soon enough the plateau would be beneath them... and not too many kilometers beyond that was a craggy mountain range with several active volcanoes.

Eliot wasn't sure who picked this landing site. He'd have a talk with them later... if there was a later.

*Icarus* didn't have the fuel for a return to orbit to try for the landing again. He had two choices: turn tail and run back up to *Hermione* on his afterburners, or find a way to bleed off some speed.

"Is everyone buckled in tight?" Eliot asked.

John looked back into the cabin, then said, "Yeah. Why?"

Eliot pulled hard on the yoke, putting the raven into a steep climb. He figured they had to be pulling three, maybe four gees. He held tight to the controls, allowing the ship to do a loop, up and over, sending hundreds of little bits of paper and wrappers from protein bars falling to the ceiling. The passengers screamed. Eliot ignored them.

He pulled *Icarus* through the loop and leveled her off again. Unfortunately, they were still going too fast.

"Hang on!"

One person in the back shouted, "No!"

Europe tilted away from them again and they looped high into the sky once more. Eliot made sure this was a bigger, taller loop. They'd have to fly upside down a little longer, but they'd definitely slow down more this time. At the tail end, he pulled them out of the loop a little early, describing a "9" in the sky, rather than a "o"; they were at a much higher altitude than before. The plateau was laid out like a map below them.

"We're almost there, folks," Eliot said. He put the raven into a series of leisurely figure eights, making full use of the thin air to slow them even further as they gently descended to the surface of the planet. The landing itself was, if anything, an anticlimax.

No one applauded.

✿

After a heated discussion about the proper way to execute a planetary landing, the other nineteen colonists agreed to let Eliot be the first to exit the raven. He slid on his pressure suit and moved into the tiny airlock. It took a couple of minutes to equalize to the pressure outside the ship.

Eliot had realized as soon as he agreed to pilot *Icarus* that he might end up being the first person to step onto the planet Europe. With only hours to prepare, he had looked to history to see what brave words others had left behind in similar situations.

Neil Armstrong stepping onto the Moon: "That's one small step for a man, one giant leap for mankind." That was the gold standard, as far as Eliot was concerned.

G. August Robinson stepping onto Mars: "Today, humanity makes a statement: we will not be confined to the surface of our small world; we will make our presence known throughout the universe." A little blustery, but not bad.

Sadie Verona stepping onto Titan: "Yeee-haw!" What she lacked in gravitas, she sure made up for in enthusiasm.

He suspected there were a couple more of those kinds of quotes that had been recorded on other worlds, back home and elsewhere, during their seventy-five year journey to Iota. He hadn't had time to request they be sent down the beam from Earth. He doubted they'd be helpful, anyway.

The pressurization cycle ended and the door of the ship opened.

There it was: the surface of Europe. Drier than the Sahara, colder than the Russian steppe, rock and dust in equal measure. Eliot knew that the other colonists would see this as a barren, inhospitable world... or as a scientific opportunity... or as a historical stepping-stone on their way to the center of the galaxy. Eliot didn't see any of that. As clear as day he saw lush, green fields of wheat blowing in a leisurely breeze. He saw rolling plains darkened by the passage of thundering bison. In the distance, over the gleaming, blue ocean, he saw thunderheads approaching with much needed rain for his crops. He saw what Earth used to be, and what Europe would become.

As he stepped off the ladder and crushed wind-carved pebbles under his boot, Eliot Burke decided that he would build his farm on this very spot.

"We're home."

# FALL

America

October 7, 3
*(December 28, 2261)*

Sally and Trent walked me to the edge of the cliff. I needed the help. My suit would have been too heavy to walk comfortably in Earth gravity. Here on America, at 1.18 g, the weight of the suit was almost unbearable. Sally had given up trying to talk me out of this. "How are you feeling?" was all she could manage.

"Great," I said. I didn't want to spoil the mood with a lot of talk. I was scared out of my mind, and more excited than I'd ever been in my life. How many people can say they were the *first* to do something? Not many. I would be one.

Trent was more obvious in his support. "This is gonna be *major*! You got your tunes?"

"Right here."

Trent, though more supportive of the basic idea, was of the opinion that this would, in the final analysis, be very boring. He insisted I take a music player with a variety of my favorite songs. I let him have his way. The player added less than a gram to the weight of the suit.

Sally and Trent were bundled against the cold. The temperature was hovering around 50 below. All I could see of them, past their oxygen masks, were their eyes. Trent

25

was smiling, I could tell. Sally was not. I wanted to give them each a hug. My pressure suit was far too bulky to get even close to a real embrace, so I patted them on their shoulders. They could see my face clearly through my plastic helmet. I showed an unconcerned smile to reassure them. Sally nodded. I nodded back.

They helped me turn to face the edge. Beyond the gray rock of the plateau, below the deep purple sky, the planet disappeared. Even the bright light of late-morning Iota could not banish the shadows of the crevasse. This cliff was higher than any on Earth. It was higher than any on Mars. It dwarfed anything in our home system by two orders of magnitude. This gash in the surface of America was the deepest known hole on any body in any system, extending from the dry sparse plateau known as the Butlerian Highlands down into the deepest part of this planet yet explored, two thousand kilometers below. Not two thousand meters. Two thousand *kilo*meters—about the distance between New York and Miami. A long way down. Someone with a dark sense of humor had named this abyss the Pit of Hades.

I ran as fast as I could for the edge and jumped.

As one of the original settlers to the Iota system, I remember the feel of Earth gravity. I grew up in it, spent most of my life in it. This immediately felt *wrong*. It was too much, as if I was falling in fast forward. For every second, the gravity of this overlarge world was pulling me eleven and a half meters per second faster. The reptilian part of my brain told me that the problem was the bulky suit, that it was dragging me down into the inky shadows of the chasm, that I should remove it and at least fall at a more reasonable rate of acceleration.

I ignored that part of my brain.

After the first minute, I was falling something like 700 meters per second.

The first several hundred kilometers of my journey were relatively safe. For some reason better understood by the geologists on this planet, this part of the canyon rim is like a ledge, the cliff face bending away as you fall. There was little chance of me hitting anything for quite some time. The far side of the crevice was over a kilometer to the east, making this only a hairline fracture in the grand scheme of things on the planet. And making it very dark as I fell farther and farther in.

Since gravity is measured in meters per second per second, it is considered a second order term in the equation of my descent. If you fall on Earth, eventually you attain a speed known as terminal velocity. This is the speed at which the drag of the air balances perfectly with the pull of gravity. You can't fall faster than that. It comes out to something like fifty meters per second. I was well acquainted with that speed, comfortable with it. Skydiving was a hobby of mine for years before I came to America. At fifty meters per second, you can watch the ground rise to meet you calmly, waiting to pull that ripcord.

I was already falling much faster than that, because the average atmosphere on America was far thinner than Earth, and at this altitude, just a few thousand meters below the Highlands, it was even less. Since the impact of drag is based on your speed, it is called a first order term. I wouldn't experience a measurable amount of drag for nearly seven minutes.

There was another first order term in this equation that did have to be considered. The atmosphere generation for the terraforming of America was conducted on the surface, to make use of solar power and for other more esoteric reasons. Every minute, thousands of tons of new oxygen and nitrogen were pumped into the slowly thickening American sky. Like a liquid, these gasses sought out the lowest levels of the planet, and there were none lower than the Pit. The currents of air from the surface into the Pit created a constant downward flow. At the top of the cliff, the impact of these currents was minimal. I outran the flow easily in the first two seconds of fall. But as I reached the five-minute mark, I knew that a changeover was going to occur.

The shape of the Pit starts as a smooth canyon, reaching from 2,500 kilometers to the north, extending 3,000 kilometers to the south. But as you descend, you see that the distant corners work their way in, funneling into a hole that gets narrower and narrower. The result is that the air flowing quite sedately from the Highlands surface is squeezed into a tighter space, and so it speeds up.

According to my calculations, after five minutes and ten seconds, the speed of the downward current would catch up to me and *add* to the effect of gravity, making me fall even faster. I expected this.

I didn't expect to feel it like a kick in the back.

I had been falling face first, trying to face the fear, but for this part of my fall, I had to change my strategy. I leaned over, put my arms to my sides, pulled my legs together, and torpedoed down. To Earth skydivers, this would seem to be madness, but I had to minimize the impact of the air rushing down on me, and this was the best way to do it.

Dozens of times back on Earth, I would race friends to the ground, daring them to assume this kind of position for as long as they could stand. It usually wasn't very long, and they would revert to an arms-out box man position for the rest of their fall. I always wanted to build up as much speed as possible.

I was more than half a million meters down, traveling at 3,500 meters per second, and accelerating. I was one quarter of the way there.

The canyon felt more like a cave by this point. I saw no light of any kind. My suit was equipped with radar, which I switched on from a button inside my right glove, under my index finger. A wire frame depiction of the rock walls on either side of me appeared on my helmet's faceplate. I knew I was still several hundred meters from the west face and still nearly a kilometer from the east, but the radar images showed them moving so fast it felt like they had to be centimeters from me. I wanted to look away, but it was very important at this stage that I keep in mind a clear picture of my surroundings.

At seven minutes and sixteen seconds, several things happened at once. For one thing, this was the halfway point, one thousand kilometers down from the Highlands. Since I'd fallen so far into the planet, and the gravity was lessened every second, this was where I crossed the threshold of Earth normal, so my acceleration was, briefly, down to a familiar 9.8 meters per second per second. Which was good, since I was falling at nearly five thousand meters per second, or in other words, a brisk 18,000 kmh. Mach 14. Fast.

As the canyon narrowed, not only did the air pouring down from the Highlands increase in speed (though at this point nowhere near as fast as I was falling), the pressure in the cavern increased quite suddenly. Here, it was close to half an atmosphere, so the effect of drag was noticeable. In fact, given my speed, it felt very similar to splashing into water back home. I was still in my bullet pose, and now it felt right, as if I were diving into the deep end of a pool, but I knew I had to again force myself to do something that felt unnatural. I had to spread my arms and legs as far as they could go, to make use of this drag. I had to slow down and I had to do it now.

But the third thing that happened at seven minutes and sixteen seconds was the most dangerous. The analogy of diving into a pool is useful to describe the initial feeling, but it soon became something more like a tropical storm. I was a bullet shot into a hurricane. The bullet keeps going, but the hurricane makes itself known by blowing this way and that, diverting the bullet's course. Not by much, maybe only a few tenths of a degree, but enough. Enough to possibly send me careening into the west face of the Pit at such an incredible speed that even the smallest bump would completely destroy my suit and me with it.

With my middle finger, I pressed a second button in my glove and my suit filled with the sounds of Jake Genovsky, my favorite songwriter. I watched the radar picture of the west wall edge closer to me as I bounced around in the maelstrom of the cavern. Jake sang about loss and grief and hope. I silently thanked Trent.

I was slowing very quickly, so quickly that my suit's temperature regulator was having a tough time keeping up with the heat caused by compression of air beneath me; I started to sweat. Everything in the suit was waterproofed, but it still felt wrong to be surrounded by technology that was getting wet. The contractor who built the suit for me couldn't believe what I was doing. He thought I was crazy. I tried to explain that I wanted to make a mark somehow. He said I would make a mark on the floor of this canyon. I laughed, still sure I could do this. He made some comment under his breath about "damn Americans". I wondered if he was referring to my countrymen from home, or everyone on this new planet. We were already getting a reputation in the system as loud-mouthed troublemakers. I guess the insult worked either way.

It was hard to estimate what my speed was by this point, since the storm was shoving me every direction, up and down as often as left and right or to and fro. It did seem more left than right, though. The west wall crept ever closer. I toggled the button next to my ring finger. Numbers representing distances in meters were superimposed on the wire frame canyon. They were hard to read, since the numbers' positions stayed constant with me as the scenery shot past and the values changed quicker than I could really register. By keeping an eye on the size of the numbers, though, I got a much better idea of the danger I was in. I knew the storm would last at least another minute, but those numbers could scroll down to one digit and I could be pounded into the rock wall in twenty seconds or less.

The contractor had asked me if I wanted airfoils or webbing or wings, something I could use to direct myself in an atmosphere. I told him no. This wasn't about *flying* to the bottom of the Pit of Hades. It was about *falling*. Did I mention I didn't have a parachute? It was about *just* falling.

I turned right, banking my arms until I was facing east. Then I bent them back, tilting forward, moving away from the wall. I should clarify; I *tried* to do these maneuvers. It was hard to even keep a box man just to stay put, let alone to twist and tilt the way I needed to. Another safety feature of the suit's radar system was a warning tone that was programmed to chime when I was within a hundred meters of anything solid. I had finally turned to the east and was trying to move forward when I heard the tone. I was so freaked out, without thinking I spun back around to look west. The numbers flashing in front of my eyes were way too low: 95, 87, 64, 45. I watched in stupid fascination as death slid toward me. I swear I saw a single digit number, either a 9 or a 6, before I put my arms out as far as I could to the side and locked my legs together, sailing away from the rock wall feet first.

Jake continued to sing to me, and I took half a second to close my eyes and try to relax. Over the music, I heard some groans from the suit's joints. It was trying to compensate for the quickly changing pressure outside, and it was taking its toll, on the suit and on me. I swallowed a dozen times to keep my ears from exploding. I knew I should have brought gum. I tried not to think about the possibility of the suit collapsing from the strain. Maybe Sally had been right. Maybe this was all just too dangerous.

At eight minutes and thirty-two seconds into the trip, the storm finally subsided. The air pressure here, at 1,400 kilometers below the surface, was about three-quarters of an atmosphere. But I was still falling at nearly Mach 12. I only had 600 kilometers more to fall. Air drag was not going to do the trick. Lessened gravity was not going to do the trick. Even with thicker atmosphere below me providing a constantly higher coefficient of drag, at this rate I was still going to hit the bottom of the chasm in about five minutes at a hair under Mach 5.

The thing about America, though, the thing about most of the planets in the Iota system is that they're pretty young. Volcanic activity is commonplace. The crust of America is very thick, thicker on average than almost any place on Earth, but there are plenty of hot spots where the heat from the initial formation of the planet is still being slowly released. Not surprisingly, the Pit of Hades is one of those places.

2,000 kilometers below the surface is very close to the mantle of this big, rugged world. The Pit is one of the best places ever found to investigate the interaction of a planet's crust and the sluggish soup of lava on which it rests. And this crust dwarfed what we had on Earth, so it was even more interesting to Iotan geologists. At twelve minutes and twenty seconds, still two hundred kilometers from the Pit's floor, and traveling over seven thousand kilometers per hour, I saw the lights of the geological survey station. They were doing some pure research, and some more practical work on the possibility of generating geothermal power. A team of six researchers lived down there for months at a time, taking America's temperature. And the readings were very high.

All that heat created something like a blast furnace, a rush of air hot enough to melt several of the more timid metals, a rush of hot air that rose to meet me, that created something like a buffer for me. It shoved at me hard from below, slowing me down. It increased my speed relative to the air almost two-fold and so it increased the impact of the drag term in the equation.

It also increased the temperature inside my suit, but that was the least of my worries.

There was no button to push to give me speed readings. I could only look down to the ground and read the distance as it decreased. The best-case scenario was that the rising hot air would slow me to the terminal velocity in this pressure (about 1.5 atmospheres) and this gravity (about .84 g) and I would land with a bone-jarring crash that wouldn't end my life.

Anything other than the best case scenario wasn't worth dwelling on. I turned off the distance indicators. I turned off the radar.

They say you can't remember pain. I don't believe that. I remember every broken bone I've ever gotten since age five when I busted my right clavicle falling off a dirt bike. I remember pain vividly. But I don't think you can remember fear. Falling that last few thousand meters to the canyon floor, I remember that I was afraid, that I was worried I might die, that I reviewed a hundred and one regrets I'd stored up in my life. But I don't really remember the fear itself, so it's hard to describe it now, I guess. Maybe I shouldn't even try.

With my pinkie, I turned on my radio. "Attention Hades Survey Team. Attention Hades Survey Team." I was glad to get a quick response.

"This is Hades. Identify."

"I'm coming down. Please keep the landing field clear."

"Who is this?"

"My name is Baxter."

"Baxter? Baxter who? Who is this?"

"You might want to come out and watch."

I turned off the radio and concentrated on Jake's voice. Now he was singing about springtime and love and happiness. The small clearing below consisted of two squat, sturdily built ceramic structures: one laboratory and one dormitory. There was also a smooth black surface painted with a fluorescent yellow circle for transport vehicle landings. The area was brightly lit by a ring of raised halogen lamps. I angled my descent for the center of the landing pad. The door of the lab opened. From this height, I could just make out two heavy suited figures with their heads tilted up. One pointed at me. Good. They could see me.

In the song, Jake concluded that spring is the best season of the year, and I crashed face down into the ground. I bounced once, and came to rest.

Someone tapped me on the shoulder. I could feel it, so I knew I was still alive. I waved a hand to show I was okay. Two people flipped me over onto my back, a man and a woman. I couldn't lie flat because of the suit's design, so I sat up and turned on my radio again. The man was yelling at me.

"—do you think you're doing?"

"I jumped down."

"You did what?"

The man was clearly angry with me. I couldn't figure out why until I realized that if I had landed on one of their buildings I might have killed the entire research team. The woman was puzzled, trying to figure out if I could be lying, or if I could be crazy.

"I jumped down. From the Highlands."

"That's not possible."

"You're probably right."

I knew people wouldn't want to believe that this was possible, let alone that I had actually done it. I was making a sensory recording, so eventually people would have to believe me. And try it themselves. I had a brief stab of guilt over what I assumed would be many dozens, maybe hundreds of people who wouldn't have as much luck as I did, especially after the planet warmed up and the atmosphere stabilized. The jump would become impossible.

I was the first to do it. Maybe the only one.

The woman helped me stand up while the man continued to fume. She smiled at me; I smiled back. One believer. Only a few thousand to go... on America, anyway.

"You should stand back now," I told them.

"Why?" the man barked. The woman was already moving off the landing pad.

"I'm going back up."

"You're not taking our shuttle! It's here in case of emergency!" The woman put a hand on the man's arm, and he paused and moved back with her. I waved to the woman and gave a cynical salute to the man. I pressed the fifth button, the one next to my thumb, the one that I had forced myself not to push a hundred times during my descent.

The rocket built into the back of my suit ignited, and I flew up from the canyon floor just as Iota came into view above to light the Pit of Hades for today's magical handful of minutes.

# STORM

Europe

February 3, 17
*(August 10, 2279)*

His father stood like a stone pillar, holding up the tarp against the wind. Martin Burke waited impatiently for the signal. His job was to run up with the staple gun and reattach each section of tarp to the metal frame that covered their plot of potatoes. This was the worst storm in their farm's sixteen-year history. Then again, every storm was the worst storm ever.

The winds fell off a little. Martin readied himself, his full attention focused on his father's left hand. With a double-tap of fingers, the man who Martin would never think of as "Eliot" beckoned his son to the pole. The boy ran up and confidently shot thick iron staples through the translucent tarpaulin and into the more pliable aluminum of the low-hanging frame. His dad sidestepped through the furrows, pulling the tarp up and onto the frame in lengths of two meters. Martin followed close, like a passenger car attached to a tram engine, securing the plastic sheeting at each predetermined anchor point.

The wind kicked up again, one gust almost pulling Martin's oxygen mask off his face. He tried to stay to continue the work, but his father shooed him away to the relative safety of a drainage culvert. Reluctant to abandon him, Martin followed his father's silent command and crouched, waiting for the next lull in the storm.

The storm had come early this year. Martin knew, even though this was only his fourth time around, that the storm arrived earlier every year. It seemed that was a necessary evil. As Europe's atmosphere thickened from the work of the terraforming stations, the storms grew more powerful. The meteorologists down in Berlin claimed that when the air reached a certain pressure, the biannual storms would become manageable artifacts of a stable planetary weather system. But it would get worse before it got better.

✿

They rested for thirty minutes at midday, when Iota stood highest in the sky and a thin sliver of Asia hung close by like a surly younger brother. During that short lunch break, Martin ventured a question he'd asked many times:

"Why don't we get a dome, Dad?"

"Soon, Martin." That was all he ever said when Martin asked about stuff like that: "soon". Sometimes "soon" turned into "now", like the time they were able to get a badly needed truckload of nitrate pellets for the potato field, or last year when they installed a new water recycling system. But often enough, "soon" sounded like "never" to Martin.

The break over, they returned to their work.

✿

Martin was famished as he pulled his chair to the table for dinner. Dad sat at the head of the table, as usual, with Mom at the other end fretting about the sparseness of the meal. Elaine sat across from Martin. She was only four. She didn't understand yet how hard it was to grow food. Martin could hear her feet swinging under her chair as they all listened to Dad say grace.

"...and we ask Your blessings on the other families around Iota working, like we are, to make this a place of peace and bounty. For Your glory, oh Lord. Amen."

"Amen," Martin breathed quietly in response. Elaine grabbed the bowl of mashed potatoes, Mom scolded her for reaching across the table, and the meal began. For several minutes, there was only the click of serving spoons on tin bowls and the scrape of forks on metal plates. Mom and Dad were too tired to talk, and Elaine was too hungry.

Martin wondered at the silence. During the storm season, days were marked by the constant howl of wind, but the nights were eerily silent. Asia continued to pull their hard-won atmosphere away on the day side of the planet, where other families now fought to repair their tarp-covered fields. Here on the night side, the air pressure was unusually low. The nights were quiet and calm and, worst of all, cold. Mending the tarps at night would have been easier without 60-kph gusts to fight against, but the Burkes didn't have heated suits to brave the chill of nights that dropped to negative fifty degrees. Nor did they have artificial lighting to work by. The glow of DeGaulle, even when it was full, wasn't enough.

Martin and his family would hole up for the night in their home under the hill, burning the castoffs from last year's crop for fuel. It had gotten to the point where Martin couldn't smell potatoes anymore.

When storm vacation ended in ten weeks, Martin would return to school down in Berlin. Most of his classmates were already counting the days until they would graduate and they could leave Europe for the cities of the Asian moons. They traded tales of computers that could talk, vehicles that were for hauling people instead of produce, and living under domes that made Berlin's look like a kid's toy. Then, in hushed tones, they discussed the Asian women, all of them tall and blonde and gorgeous.

Martin joined in with the others, reveling in talk of exotic, faraway places. But he also loved Europe and the family farm. He didn't know if he wanted to leave, or if he would rather stay to help his dad build something special, something for the family to be proud of. His thoughts returned again and again to that question.

After dinner, Martin's father would retreat to his study—a room deep under the hill in the back of their home, no bigger than a closet—where he listened to the radio. Berlin had two stations: one for weather and agricultural news, and the other for wider news of the Iota system. During storm season, both stations went on a night-only schedule, since everyone on the Berlin Plateau was out working during the day.

Dad sat, hunched in his beat-up old metal chair, worrying the dial back and forth, trying to outsmart the crackling interference of cosmic rays. Martin stood in the doorway, not quite sneaking up on his dad, but not announcing himself, either. It was times like this that Martin almost—not quite, but almost—thought of his father as a person like any other. This gruff, sensible man had lived an entire life before Martin was born. When he was a boy, he had needs and wants like anyone else.

A story about the Council in Bombay working out the prices for next year's crop ended. Martin sensed his dad's increased interest as the announcer reviewed a collection of headlines that came down the beam from Earth.

That was the main difference between them, Martin thought. His dad grew up on a completely different planet, one that Martin would probably never visit. What must it have been like to live in a place where you could go outside without a mask? Where there were bodies of water deep enough that you might drown? Where the fields were green and the sky was blue instead of Europe's endless tan-on-tan? Even the year was different, only about three hundred fifty days, instead of the four-hundred-sixty-three-and-a-half of Europe. It was all they could do to prepare for a season now. How much harder would it be to farm on Earth, where the seasons were so much shorter?

It wasn't that Martin felt like his dad regretted leaving Earth. He clearly liked Europe and he loved his farm; he loved it almost as much as he loved his family. But Dad remembered things about Earth fondly, and missed the details.

He let those thoughts out at the most unusual times. Just today, out of nowhere during a lull in the storm, he had said, "I miss cellos."

"What are cellos?" Martin had asked.

"Musical instruments. Strings on a wooden body."

That made Martin laugh, the idea of a body made of wood. Dad laughed with him, then the storm kicked in, and they didn't discuss it again. Afterward, Martin seemed to think that his laughing might have hurt his dad's feelings. He wasn't sure.

"In the world of sport," the announcer said, "the Metropolitan Yankees defeated the Tucson Cubs in Game 6 of the World Series of Baseball last evening, ending the series. The final result was Metropolitan with four games to Tucson's two."

"Damn it!" Dad yelled. The shout from his father made Martin knock his elbow against the door to the study. Dad turned around.

"I didn't know you were there," he said.

"I'm sorry."

"It's okay. Just listening to the radio."

"What made you so mad?"

"What?" Dad seemed genuinely confused by the question, then he understood and laughed. Martin took an unconscious step closer to his father. "It's just an old sports team I used to follow. I'm not mad. How could I be? They never win."

"But then why do you follow them?"

"I guess... I guess it's because they never stop trying."

The way he looked at Martin... it was strange and new to the boy. It was almost as if Dad was talking to Martin like an adult. It made him feel grown up. He thought it was just a nice moment with his dad.

They listened to the rest of the news, then called it a night.

Martin didn't notice that was the moment he stopped wondering about his life choices.

✧

Weeks later, when school started and he and all of his classmates were signing up for their classes, Martin chose several courses in the agricultural track. He didn't remember that short conversation with his father... except that, really, he did.

# SPRING

Africa

April 23-24, 24
*(February 19-20, 2289)*

Harlan slid open the door of the shuttle. He caught a whiff of the air outside before the doors of the shuttle bay clanged shut overhead. It was an odd smell, heavy. Just enough of it slipped past his oxygen mask to put him in mind of somewhere far off, like the Caribbean, or Morocco, or some other place he'd never been. He tipped his hat to the pilot for the smooth ride and carried his duffel into the city along with the ten other passengers who came in on the flight.

The shuttle bay was all gleaming metal and smooth plastic, but like an unwanted stepchild, it was walled off from the rest of Bouyain Village. Through the airlock, taking off his mask, Harlan came into the main city. Some of his fellow travelers met family or friends. Harlan expected some sort of greeting, but no one held a sign saying "H. Branshear".

He'd never been to the planet known as Africa before, but he was fully briefed on Bouyain Village. He knew the population was three thousand. He knew that the industrial base was almost nonexistent. And he knew where the local ABRS facility was, so that's the way he went, brushing past many pedestrians.

Covered by a dome made up of thousands of clear plastic pentagons, the village was less than one square kilometer in size, and it was crammed with buildings. Some few, those nearest the shuttle bay, were built in something like a modern style, but it seemed that the steel had run out quickly. The rest of the village seemed to be built almost entirely of some sort of dark wood. Harlan paused to examine the wall of one home. The material was an odd color, grayish, and the grain was too fine to see without peering at it closely. He tapped it. It seemed strong. A man came out of the house and looked Harlan up and down.

"Can I help you?"

Harlan assumed his uniform was off-putting to this local, so he tried to be as polite as possible.

"No, sir. Just admiring the workmanship."

"Well then."

Harlan had been dismissed. "Thanks for your time," Harlan said, and continued on his way.

The city was almost devoid of technology, or at least technology that was obvious. The streets weren't awash in litter and filth, so something was keeping them clean. There were no cars or trains. Everyone seemed to walk. After ten years posted on bustling Gandhi, it felt odd.

The office of the African Biological Research Society was another gray-wood building, this one imposing rather than quaint. A directory in the lobby showed Harlan where to find Dr. Olivia Kim, Associate Professor of Relational Biology: office 214. Harlan found the office and knocked. A petite young Asian woman opened the door. She was dressed for an excursion, wearing a backpack, covered head to toe in a body suit that was almost the same color as the office walls.

"You're a man."

"I see they don't give degrees in biology to just anyone." Harlan smiled at her and offered his hand. She didn't smile back and she didn't shake his hand.

"Come in."

The room was small, tidy, empty of personality. Harlan

was suddenly not looking forward to the next three days.

"Lt. Colonel Harlan Branshear, reporting for duty." He considered giving her a little salute, but thought the better of it.

"Should I call you Lieutenant?"

"No, I'm a Lt. Colonel. I'm not in the Navy."

"Well then, Colonel, the reason I—"

"I'm not a Colonel, either, ma'am. Why don't you just call me Harlan?"

"And I expect you'll want to call me Olivia."

"Or Liv?" Her unamused look told Harlan the answer to that.

"The problem is that I requested a woman."

"I'm not sure I see how that's relevant."

Harlan set down his duffel. Olivia eyed it, annoyed. She still wore her backpack and was clearly ready to leave.

"Men and women send out very different kinds of pheromones. Most of the researchers who go into the wild from this station are women. The local wildlife are used to our scent and you'll throw off the tenuous equilibrium we've managed up to now."

"Personnel are hard to come by, lately. I was tapped to help out on this mission."

"Mission... Fine. How long will you need to get ready?"

Harlan picked up the duffel again and slung it over his shoulder with a flourish.

"No." Olivia moved to the desk and picked up a telephone. Harlan grinned at the device. Telephones were already considered antiquated on Gandhi. "This is Dr. Kim. I need a field suit for a man, size..."

"Thirty-six."

"Thirty-six. Thank you."

She hung up. Harlan put down the duffel again. He waited, but Olivia didn't seem inclined to offer any explanation.

"Why do I need a field suit?" he asked.

"You've never been in the African wilds."

"Not these African wilds. Why?"

"You need the protection. Bare skin is an invitation to

disaster."

"Oh... Why?"

"Trust me."

Olivia sat down at her desk and started typing something on her computer. Harlan was, for the moment, forgotten, so he took a look at Olivia's bookshelf. Books were hard to come by on the Asian moons. Almost any information you needed was available on the net. The few things that weren't could be requested over the beam from Earth. It looked like a computer, even a relic like Olivia's, was a luxury on Africa, so there were books. About half were fading, musty tomes, carried all the way from Earth on *Hermione*; the other half were locally produced. Differentiating the two was easy; the local books were bound not in leather or cardboard, but in more of that grayish wood, which seemed odd to Harlan. He pulled one from the shelf without checking the title. The pages were white, but not quite paper. Something manufactured, like plastic, but more pliable. The spine and front and back covers were sanded smooth, like the top of a coffee table, the title etched into the front panel.

"Hm."

"Excuse me?" Olivia asked.

"Oh. Sorry. I was just looking at some of your books."

"We'll be leaving in a few minutes."

"Okay."

Harlan put the book back in its place and moved to another wall with a map of the city and its immediate surroundings. It put him in mind of those fifteenth- and sixteenth-century maps of the New World. The details grew sparse at a distance from the town. The map showed little more than topographical features. A hill here, a ravine there. He noticed there were no bodies of water.

"What do they drink?" he asked. This made Olivia look up. He didn't have to explain that his question had to do with the local wildlife.

"Why do you ask?"

"The map. No lakes or streams. Is there a local water source?"

She looked at him carefully, sizing him up. Something about the question had made her suspicious. In the end, he expected she would decide to trust him. People in their twenties can't imagine someone over sixty as anything but a likeable old fool. That's why Harlan never died his hair.

"We're going to look for a local spring. It's a day from here, to the northeast."

"A day from here? Not very precise."

"Distance is hard to measure in the wild."

She returned to work. This was getting ridiculous. Harlan dropped into a chair and leaned toward the desk.

"So, are you Korean?"

"I was born and raised on Africa."

"No, I mean... Never mind."

The first generation of locals didn't have any idea how many things they had lost by being born fifty-six light years from Earth. Each day, Harlan had to decide all over again if that was good or bad. He wasn't sure yet today.

After ten very quiet minutes, an assistant arrived with Harlan's suit. Five minutes after that, they left the office for the North Exit of Bouyain Village. Walking through the streets dressed like a researcher, Harlan felt more at home with the locals. There were a wide variety of ethnic types represented, though that only seemed noteworthy to someone like Harlan who remembered Earth; he was a "preemie" in the current lingo. He had said more than once that he'd like to find the person who changed the definition of that word and give him (or her) a smack. Of course, that just made him sound more like a preemie.

The wall at the edge of the village was high, over ten meters. Nothing of the terrain or wildlife beyond was visible. Harlan felt the tension starting to build. He had seen precious little out the window of the shuttle coming in, only dense forest. Sensories of African journeys were difficult to come by, even for a Lt. Colonel in the Iotan Army. The bottom line was that he didn't know what to expect. Olivia led him to the airlock. They walked into the small chamber.

Olivia started to pull her masked hood over her head

when Harlan put a hand on her arm. She didn't appreciate the gesture.

"We need to talk," he said.

"I know. I'll save you the trouble."

"Really?"

"You were going to give me the lecture about how you're the boss and what you say goes. If we're ten meters from our goal and you decide it's too risky to continue, we turn around immediately and I don't argue. Something like that?"

"Well, yeah."

"It's not like that here. I'm in charge." Harlan's temper cracked a little. Olivia held up a hand. "I know more about what's on the other side of that door than anyone alive, and you know *nothing*. Am I right?"

Harlan nodded slowly.

"If there is something out of the ordinary, a seismic event, a medical emergency, a sudden storm, then, yes, I will defer to you... but anything to do with the wild itself? I'm the expert, I'm the lead, I dictate what happens and how. I requested backup because it is standard procedure, but it is not an opportunity for you, it is a responsibility for you, and I define where your responsibilities begin and end. Is that clear?"

Harlan paused. "That's quite a speech."

"I've given it before."

More silence filled the little room.

"Anything to do with the wild, you're the boss. Otherwise..."

Olivia nodded. She pulled her hood up. Only her eyes were visible now, through plastic goggles built into the suit, but they still said volumes about her opinion of Harlan and her estimation of his worth. He grinned as he pulled on his own hood. Olivia opened the door.

The light was bright, so he didn't see much at first, but the smell hit him like a roundhouse. It was like the smell he sensed in the shuttle bay, but many times stronger. He was reminded of curry, but that wasn't quite right. It was definitely a spicy sort of smell. The mask he wore wasn't designed to filter the local atmosphere, which was nontoxic to humans, merely to provide him with the oxygen that Africa lacked.

It was also cold; he estimated at least ten degrees below freezing. He hoped the gray bodysuit would be warm enough. Olivia walked out, and Harlan followed.

The first thing he saw as his eyes grew used to the daylight was that the ground was moving. He could feel it under his boots, shifting and pulsing. He looked down and saw that the ground was that same color that he was starting to think of as African Gray. As he looked at it closer, he saw that he wasn't really standing on ground. It was a writhing mass of creatures. Some were long and round, python or boa size. Others were flatter, scuttling like beetles. Many worms slithered in between. Other stranger shapes, more geometrical: bugs shaped like squares and hexagons. Thinking he'd walked in the wrong place, Harlan sidestepped to the left, but it was more of the same. To the right. Forward. Everywhere. He looked at Olivia in alarm.

"That's the ground. There's no soil," she said.

"No soil? Rocks?"

"Not that we've found. Obviously there's a planetary crust somewhere underneath, but biomass is all we've seen so far on this planet."

Harlan was fascinated as well as revolted. The flat no-man's-land between the high walls of Bouyain Village and the beginning of the jungle was a sea of living (breathing?) life. And, most importantly, it seemed to ignore him.

"Am I hurting anything?"

"Probably. But if you do crush a nematode or a crustacean, it will be eaten by something else. Nothing is wasted. Come on." Olivia trudged forward through the muck toward the trees that marked the edge of the wilds. Harlan followed, wary. The trees weren't very tall, not even five meters as an average, but they sported a very thick canopy of leaves. The leaves were a little greener than African Gray, but still nothing like an oak or an elm. There was more strange geometry to them, too. They looked like some computer model of a leaf where the designer couldn't quite get the fractals right.

The trunks of the trees were almost metallic, very cylindrical and smooth. No knots that Harlan could see, at least not in the few he walked under as he followed Olivia. He knocked on one with a knuckle, and was disappointed when the tree didn't ring like a bell.

The canopy made the jungle dark, dimmer than twilight. Olivia hadn't turned on a lamp, so Harlan followed her lead. Deeper into the wild, the smell got heavier, which Harlan hadn't thought possible. He also wasn't pleased to see that the floor creatures were slithering and skittering their way up each and every tree trunk. There was so much movement all around him, and all of it in minute shades of the same dull color; his eyes began to feel the strain of sorting out this troublesome data.

"It's hard to see."

"Don't turn on your lamp."

"I know. It's not that it's dark; it's hard to *see*. You know what I mean?"

"You get used to it."

When? After three years of field study, Harlan guessed. He focused on the clear, unwrithing shape of his guide. She hiked with a steady, comfortable pace. Maybe defining the journey as "a day" wasn't so ridiculous after all.

"So what's dangerous out here?" he asked.

"Everything."

"Okay, I'm scared. Well done. But are there any big carnivores? Dinosaurs or something?"

"Nothing here is as evolved as that. The Bouyain trees are the most sophisticated living thing we've found yet."

"Bouyain trees, huh? Only find them in these parts?"

"Only find them around Bouyain."

"What are these?" Harlan pointed to the trees ahead.

"Different."

Harlan took a closer look. What he could see of their trunks, behind the profusion of crawling and sliding creatures, did look a little different. The grain was a little wider, and the leaves seemed different, too, almost square.

"They're similar."

"Yes."

A tree to the left was wrapped like a barber pole by a snake as thick as Harlan's leg. He couldn't see the creature's head, didn't even know if it was up above the leaves, sunning itself, or down in the soup, feeding. Something about the snake's skin seemed odd. It had a diamond pattern of scales... Harlan thought back to the first snake he'd seen, the one he'd stepped on. It looked like it was the same size, and the scales looked the same, but the first one had been striped. Harlan was almost sure. The stripes were hard to see because they were a change in texture, not in color. But he knew they weren't diamonds.

"How many species are there here?"

"Species is not a valid concept on Africa."

"What?" Harlan stepped up his pace so he could walk at Olivia's side. "There are thousands right here, it looks like."

"No, there are trillions. On Earth, *species* was defined as a collection of creatures that can interbreed. That made sense on Earth because the points on the evolutionary trail that led to viable life were few and far between. There were marmosets and there were humans. None of the steps in between survived, and marmosets and humans couldn't mate."

"You know, there are still plenty of people and marmosets on Earth. You don't have to use the past tense."

Olivia ignored his rebuke. "All life was neatly partitioned into clumps of genetically similar beings. But what would it be like if there were millions of creatures, spanning the gap between a marmoset and a human? You could breed any two of them if they were close enough on the path of evolution. You couldn't define a species the same way."

"That's what's happening here? We're seeing all the evolutionary steps at once."

"I suppose you could simplify it that way. We deal in a fuzzy version of biology that's not about classification but relation."

"Relational biology. I get it. So what's different here? Why aren't any species dying out?"

"That's not the question. Remember, there are no species." She patted a tree as she walked, almost like a pet. "Each angiosperm is its own living experiment. The question isn't why they aren't dying. They are. All the time. You're killing some right now."

Harlan was reminded of the mat of life he was walking across. Looking down, he noted that the collection of creatures already seemed very different from what was near the airlock this morning. The flat beetles had given way to spidery contraptions with seven legs and an ungraceful gait. The worms were few and far between, replaced by something more like leathery jellyfish.

"So then what's the question?" he asked.

"The question is, why are they evolving so *fast*? But the answer is easy. Radiation."

"Radiation?" Harlan was shocked out of his biology lesson. He hadn't been in active service during the war in Brazil, before *Hermione* left Earth, but he had friends that were. Many of them hadn't survived a year after exposure to nuclear fallout.

"You've had your DNA capped, right?" Olivia asked.

"Yes. That's standard practice for soldiers. But still—"

"It's standard practice for African researchers as well. You're safe. The wildlife here is suited to an environment of constant solar radiation ten hours every day, but it's not immune. Every generation spawns demonstrable changes. We don't call them Bouyain trees because they live near Bouyain Village. We made them."

"You made them? You've been tampering with the—"

"No. We didn't engineer them. We built the city. We disturbed the environment. Every creature living within fifty meters of the city has adapted to the peculiarities of living close to a human settlement. The heat we generate, the gasses we expel, the radio waves—none of these things are deadly, but they have an impact. We're having an impact right now, walking to the spring."

"I've been meaning to ask you. How do you know the spring is there?"

"Research."

"Yeah, that's great. Thanks. And I was worried we were on a wild goose chase."

Olivia was clearly annoyed, but not enough to stop walking. Harlan had to admire her for that.

"We have done careful analysis of the relative moisture content levels of the local wildlife, tracking them in many directions from the village. We have also tagged a few hundred animals and tried to determine their migratory habits, but that has been only a marginal success. Still, all the evidence indicates the presence of a spring that way." She pointed to make herself clear.

"Why not just take satellite pictures?"

Olivia waved a hand at the ceiling of leaves. Harlan looked up, noting that the leaf shapes here were more like notched ovals.

"There are other kinds of analysis you can do other than ordinary light. With radar—"

"With radar, you'd get nowhere."

Harlan was starting to think that he was getting so frustrated with Olivia that he was seeing spots, but there were some sorts of little creatures flying around in front of his face. He tried to wave them away; it did no good.

"We call them mites, but they really have little in common with Earth arachnids. In fact, they don't have legs."

"Where'd they come from?" Harlan was having a difficult time not swatting at these things, but he knew he'd just look like a fool if he did.

"They don't like the area around the village. There are plenty of things that don't like the area around the village."

"So it's going to get worse."

She nodded. He thought he saw the hint of a smile in her eyes. Maybe she did have a sense of humor stuffed away inside all that precocious blather.

They stopped at midday, after two hours of hiking. Since there were no rocks or tree stumps, Olivia merely took a seat on the "ground".

"How can you do that?" he asked.

"Do what?"

"Sit there."

This area had nothing like the pythons near the village. That niche seemed to be filled by armies of twenty-centimeter-long tank-like bugs with, Harlan tried to count, twelve double-jointed legs. He didn't see a head on the creature. One of these brutes skittered toward Olivia and Harlan almost shouted to her, but it took a right turn when it got near her and burrowed down into the muck on some unspeakable mission.

"They don't have eyes, do they?"

"No. The solar radiation isn't forgiving to optical nerves, so nothing here relies on light."

"That's why it's all the same color. There's no point in differentiating, so Mother Nature didn't bother."

Olivia nodded. She lifted her hood enough to take a sip from a water bottle, then tossed the bottle to Harlan, quickly lowering the hood again. He mimicked her, and returned the bottle. He was tired, but he still couldn't bring himself to sit down, especially with those tank-bugs roaming around.

"Why does radar get you nowhere?"

"What?"

"Earlier. You said radar gets you nowhere?"

"The leaves bounce it, scatter it everywhere."

"The leaves?"

Before looking up, Harlan tried to guess what sort of leaves he'd see this time. He imagined a Y-shape with little spikes. He was disappointed to see something like a blocky maple leaf.

"They're loaded with metals. Indium, gallium, silver, gold, palladium—"

"Silver and gold?"

"Yes. This planet, the whole system is lousy with them," Olivia said. If she knew the value those metals had on Earth, she didn't show it.

"But no iron."

"How'd you know that?"

"I was told a compass is useless here. No magnetic field."

"That's right. A little more iron and some lead, and maybe the radiation wouldn't have such an effect on the plants and animals here."

"That or oxygen in the atmosphere," Harlan suggested.

Olivia didn't like something about that comment. She stood up, bracing herself on the rough shell of one of the tank-bugs. The little beast seemed annoyed, but unhurt. It scurried away. And so did Olivia. Harlan was left to follow, wondering why mentioning oxygen was a sore point.

There were groups on all the worlds around Iota that thought Africa was being wasted. They were radical types, far from the center of any political party. Most people accepted the rules of colonization without question. To Harlan, it seemed ludicrous to agree to be frozen for seventy-five years and brought to an entirely new star if you weren't on board with the program. And rule number one was, essentially, "Thou shalt not destroy local life." Obviously some trees and worms and tank-bugs were killed to build Bouyain City, but they weren't destroyed as a species. (Well, maybe they were, but Harlan didn't want to focus on a technicality.) Rule number one made it clear that Africa wouldn't be terraformed.

News from other systems was watched with polite disinterest by most everyone around Iota; Harlan knew that one other stellar colonization ship had to *turn around* when it found all the habitable zone planets in the target system were already teeming with life. That was going to be an unhappy bunch of people when they got back home. And that star was farther from Earth than Iota. Their round trip would eventually take over two hundred years.

There was a question on the form that everyone had filled out when they applied for a berth on *Hermione*. The question was asked before placement on any of the colonization ships. It read, "In the event of a mission failure, do you wish to be revived on Earth upon return, or given priority berthing on the next outgoing colonization ship?" Harlan had chosen "priority berthing." When he woke up, he wanted it to be away from Earth, wherever (or whenever) that might be. In a moment of idle curiosity a few years ago, he had accessed the *Hermione*'s records. What was left of her was still revolving around Asia, at a prudent distance from all the Asian moons, sleeping peacefully, waiting in case another journey was required. Harlan broke *Hermione*'s security easily enough and queried the files of the colonists to find out the most common answer to that question on the form.

Eight-five percent asked to be revived on Earth if something went wrong. These were not people who gave up on the idea of *home* very easily.

What Harlan didn't know, and in fact the Iotan Army didn't know either, was how many of the people currently calling for the terraforming of Africa were preemies, and how many were native Iotans. Harlan thought that was a very important question.

Maybe oxygen was a sore point because it would be the first change in a terraforming effort on this planet, a change that would kill every form of local life as quickly and efficiently as if Earth had been smothered in carbon monoxide. Probably more efficiently.

Harlan rushed to catch up with Olivia. He found himself swatting at flying things more often. The mites were still there, but they were now joined by larger bugs that looked a little like flying chick-burs. He couldn't see wings or antennae or heads, but each of these little creatures was covered in spikes. He realized that he had dozens of them already snagged on his suit, and he couldn't brush them off. Shoving at them just moved them around.

Olivia noticed Harlan's concern. "We have a spray. We'll get rid of them before we camp. Keep moving."

"Sure thing."

Harlan felt the chick-burs edging under his duffel and tried to ignore them.

Something about the way ahead was confusing to Harlan's eyes. He was, he had to admit, getting used to seeing an ever-shifting world painted in very delicate shades of one color, but there was a fog ahead. Or maybe some sort of heat illusion? That didn't seem likely in the subfreezing air. Olivia stopped, so he stopped. He ran a hand over his mask, in case it had fogged up. It was like there was nothing beyond where they stood. A line in the jungle was the demarcation point of oblivion.

"I didn't know there was a wall out here," Olivia said, clearly annoyed. She took off her backpack and sat on the ground, dejected.

"A wall?" Like any optical illusion, once the trick was revealed the picture became clear. Harlan realized what he was seeing. It was a wall, its top just higher than Harlan's reach. It was roughly finished but sturdily built, a little thicker at the base than the top, which was rounded. He could imagine something like this in a primitive village on Earth, built from lime and mud and straw. The scale was impressive. It extended straight as an arrow right across their path as far as he could see in either direction.

"I don't get it," he said. "I though you only built villages here."

"We didn't build this. No one built this. It's alive."

"What?"

Harlan took a tentative step back, almost tripping over a thick-bodied scuttler shaped like an equilateral triangle and sporting somewhere around thirty legs. The scuttler picked up speed and ran, away from Harlan and away from the wall.

"Can it hurt us?"

"No," Olivia said, "but it is a problem."

The wall still looked manufactured to Harlan, even after he knew it was a living thing. He walked up to it, inspecting its surface, which was kind of like stucco, clearly random in design, but so uniformly random that he could imagine a painter toiling for hours to get the look just right. He touched it with his index finger... and his finger stuck.

"Olivia?"

She looked up, now concerned. "I didn't say to *touch* it!"

Harlan pulled, but the fabric of his glove was glued to the wall. He put his other hand flat against the wall to get better purchase.

"Don't!" But Olivia was too late. The leverage did no good, and now Harlan had both hands welded to the wall. "Be still! I don't want you trying to push off with your foot now."

"Fine. How do I get out of this? What's this thing going to do to me?"

"It's going to digest you for a few years. You have to take off your gloves... carefully! If you get bare skin on that thing, it's not going to be pretty."

The first glove came off easily. As he pulled his hand out, the glove flapped down and remained plastered on the wall. His other hand was tougher. He had to wiggle his fingers back and forth for a good minute before he was free. He backed off quickly.

"So the phrase 'Can it hurt us?' has some other meaning for you?"

Olivia was searching through her pack. "Put your hands under your arms."

"It's cold, but—"

"Do it!"

Harlan was about to follow her instructions when something landed on his left hand. It was almost a butterfly. It had a short, thin body and four feathery antennae. The wings were different, though, not the graceful ear-shape that he remembered from swallowtails and monarchs. These were right triangles. It was as if a translucent square, hinged down the middle, was sunning itself on his hand. The wings beat slowly. This was the first thing Harlan had seen on the planet that wasn't unsettling or frightening or hideous.

"It's cute."

"It's going to bite you." Harlan's right hand, almost of its own volition, reached up to smack the little bug, but Olivia added, "You'll die if you kill it."

"Okay, what are you—" The creature, with teeth or claws or something else even more baroque that Harlan couldn't see, bit into the back of his hand. It was painful. Gunshot painful. Migraine painful. It took every ounce of his strength to not bat the thing away. It was difficult to remain standing. Olivia waited, holding the spare gloves she'd found.

After three seconds, the butterfly released its grip and

flew off. Olivia rushed over and covered Harlan's hands. The pain seemed to fade very quickly.

"Explain." Harlan was starting to lose his patience with this world.

"It sensed your smell, it landed, it tasted you, it didn't like how you tasted, it left. Keep covered from here on out."

"Why shouldn't I have just killed it!? If this is about saving the damn creatures, I'll—"

"If you had killed it, the others would have smelled its death, and they would have attacked you, suit or not. And they wouldn't care how you tasted."

"The others?"

Harlan looked around, stunned to realize that there were thousands of the flittering squares above him, floating in and out of the tree leaves above. In fact, the leaves here were a triangular shape similar to the butterflies' wings. If he didn't know what he was looking for, he would have assumed it was simply a windy day.

"They're a colony? A hive?"

"Not really. It's very basic instinctual behavior. They don't seem to cooperate in any other way. Of course, we could be missing something, but we don't think they're as social as bees or ants."

"Uh-huh. That's great. If you're worried about too many people coming here and wrecking the planet, just tell them about those guys."

"It's all in the literature, if you had bothered to read it."

Harlan paused, listening.

"What?" Olivia asked.

Harlan shushed her and did a slow spin. Something had caught his attention. Some sound that shouldn't have been there. Something human. Another faint whisper of conversation drifted to him. It came from the southwest, along the wall. He gestured for Olivia to follow him, quietly. Thirty meters along, he saw them. A man and a woman, dressed like Harlan and Olivia; they were doing something to the wall. They didn't seem to be concerned about making noise, so Harlan bent into a crouch and moved closer.

Whoever these people were, they were prepared. The

woman carried something like a rolled up carpet and placed it against the wall near the jungle floor. She carefully unspooled it upward, keeping it straight, making sure there were no gaps. When it was flat against this side of the wall, held in place by the wall's sticky surface, she gave it a shove, sending the rest of the carpet rolling up and over the top. She pressed a button on the side of the carpet. Hand and foot holds sprouted from the surface of the mat.

"Clever," Harlan whispered.

"I don't know them," Olivia said.

The man, a large fellow, broad shouldered, muscular, wearing a colossal backpack, climbed up the wall using the silver holds. He sat astride the wall, looking down on the other side. He gave the woman a thumbs up and climbed down out of sight. The woman followed him up and over the wall.

Harlan and Olivia waited for a minute or so, then moved up to the makeshift climbing surface.

"They're headed for the spring," Olivia said.

"How do you know that?"

"They have to be from Bouyain Village. The nearest settlement is a thousand kilometers away. And for them to be traveling this close to our path is too much of a coincidence."

Harlan thought about it for a second. "You're right."

"We have to stop them," Olivia said.

"Why?"

"They aren't with the ABRS; they must be energy scouts."

"Energy scouts? You make this stuff up as you go, don't you?" Harlan asked.

"Do I have to spell everything out for you? What do you think this spring is?"

"A place where animals drink. Water comes up out of the ground."

"I never said there was water here," Olivia said.

"You said you tracked water levels in the local animals."

"I said I tracked moisture levels. There is no water on Africa."

"That's not possible."

"There is a hundred times more biomass on this planet than Earth. Very few things here live to more than five or six years old."

"You mean Africa years or Europe years?" Harlan asked. He knew enough about her now to assume she didn't mean Earth years.

"It doesn't matter. Don't get sidetracked. That's a lot of things living and dying all the time. What do you think the lower layers of the planet are like under us?"

"Gray."

"I told you all we've ever seen of Africa is living matter. Even the village foundations were set down on the felled trees of the initial survey teams. Deep down, under us, is layer after layer of dead biological matter, pressed and crushed by the weight of the living. What's going to spring up out of that?"

Harlan felt a shiver of realization.

"Oil."

☼

The tent was made of more of the same odor-free gray fabric as their suits, pressurized with oxygen and heated to a little above freezing with a few chemical packs. Olivia said building a fire was out of the question.

They had a light meal of oatmeal and warm water while Harlan tended to the bite on his hand. Olivia had originally struck Harlan as quiet, perhaps even stoic. But once her "secret" was out, he could barely get a word in edgewise.

"It's the biggest threat facing the Iotan system!"

"That's an overstatement," Harlan said.

"An overstatement? You realize that siphoning the oil off this planet will destroy the entire ecosystem?"

"First, the ecosystem on this planet is important, sure, but not in the scope of things in the whole system. Second, they were pretty good at getting the oil out of the ground without messing up nature too much when I left Earth.

59

They kind of had to be."

"That was more than a hundred years ago. We have fusion now."

"We don't have fusion around Iota. No fuel."

"Fine, but we do have fission. And, yes, someday we'll run out of uranium. So we need to work on alternate energy sources, like anti-matter."

"For Iota, oil *is* an alternate source," he said. "And you say there are trillions of gallons of it, everywhere on this planet, right under our feet. What's the harm in dropping a pipe from orbit and pumping it to tankers in space? You'd need very little infrastructure down here."

Olivia handed him a tray of oatmeal, which Harlan ate quickly, without tasting it.

"It's the first nudge in a spiraling orbit. You'll need a small team to watch the pipe and conduct repairs. You'll need a support staff to maintain their habitat. You'll need a biological team to keep the African animals from disrupting the flow of oil. You'll need a hospital and a clerical staff and a restaurant and a barber and—"

"I get it. I still don't see the big deal."

"How long will it be before there are so many people here, and so much investment in this planet, that they'll be able to terraform?"

"They can't," Harlan said.

"Why?"

"The Treaty that we all signed before we came here."

"I didn't sign it," Olivia said.

Harlan was stumped, once again caught thinking like a preemie. He really was a generation behind in his thinking. Native Iotans barely knew what the Treaty was. He wiped the tray clean and handed it back to Olivia. She had already eaten, so she put away the supplies.

"Get some rest. We've got work tomorrow," she said

"I don't know..."

"We have to stop them." She wasn't lecturing now. She wasn't demanding. Harlan saw fear in her eyes for the first time. A million and one ways to die on this planet didn't faze her, but this...

"That's not what I mean," he said. "I should check on our friends. Make sure they're still in their tent." He started to put his mask back on.

"You should stay here in the tent while it's dark out." Now she was lecturing again.

He caught himself unconsciously rubbing the bandage on his hand.

"Okay."

Olivia was already climbing into her sleeping bag. Harlan watched her for a moment. She was a pretty girl, he had to admit, and now, concerned for her livelihood and her world, she was more human, more accessible. Somewhere in the back of his brain, he thought he should be attracted to her, that this was the kind of thing that happened in books or movies. The tender love scene before the big shoot out the next day. Somewhere closer to the front of his brain, Harlan accepted the fact that he was old enough to be her father. He could be her grandfather. Come to think of it, with all the time he'd spent frozen on *Hermione*, he could add a couple or three *great*s to that grandfather title.

The other option, of course, was for him to bond with her like she was his daughter. Forty years (plus or minus seventy-five) in the armed forces had left Harlan with no wife, no children, no personal commitments that outlived the length of a posting. He would protect her and guide her and she would appreciate and love him unconditionally.

Harlan couldn't help laughing a little at himself. Olivia was already asleep and didn't hear him. He crawled into his bag fairly sure that he and Olivia would stay what they were: scientist and soldier.

✿

"Are they still going the right way?" Harlan asked under his breath. Olivia nodded. According to her, they would reach the spring in two hours. Ahead, Nick and Nora kept a steady pace through the jungle. Olivia had asked Harlan why he decided to call them that. He refused to tell her, which she found infuriating. Harlan liked the small pleasures in life.

In the early light of dawn, the wild seemed dim and threatening. Iota snuck through the treetops in patches over their right shoulders. This far away from Bouyain Village, the impact of humanity was nonexistent and there was more life around than Harlan had thought possible. The mites were legion, and butterflies, these sporting a hexagonal shape, filled the sky overhead. Larger flying creatures zipped by too fast to see clearly. Harlan had caught a glimpse of one that was circular, the size of a Frisbee, but hollow: a flying ring. Another was shaped remarkably like an orbital plane he remembered from Earth called a Concorde. Both analogies would have been lost on Olivia.

The ground had changed as well. It seemed less stable, undulating in a slow but perceptible rhythm. The feeling that he was inside some giant beast, carried along by peristalsis, overwhelmed Harlan. There was still the writhing mass of worms and beetles and new tiny little things very much like maggots, everything still that dark, steely gray color. The walk was complicated by the appearance of something new, whether plant or animal, Harlan didn't know, which floated along close to the ground. They resembled seaweed, thin to transparency, ribbons of alternating rough and smooth texture. They weighed almost nothing, carried on the slow, fragrant wind. Harlan's progress wasn't impeded. He could walk right through these weeds, but they did eventually build up as a gummy muck on his boots and ankles.

He tried to focus on Nick and Nora, since they were his biggest concern, but he was being continuously distracted by the carnage going on around him. However the animals had been eating yesterday, it was either too subtle to notice or hidden from view. Not anymore. Boa-sized snakes were pouncing on beetles, cobra-like in their speed. But the snakes weren't immune from attack. One of the Concordes pierced a boa-cobra in the neck, with a meaty slicing sound. That wasn't the worst of it. The worst was the sound the arrow-shaped Concorde made as it sucked the life out of the boa-cobra. Harlan was glad to leave that little scene behind, not eager to see what the rest of the crowd would do with the body of the snake.

Olivia put a hand on Harlan's arm, warning him to stop. She saw something ahead, something Harlan couldn't see. And neither, based on their unchanged pace, could Nick or Nora.

"The spring," she whispered, pointing straight ahead. "It's up there."

"How do you know?"

"The trees are thinning out."

Harlan took her word for it, and they trudged on. Olivia was getting antsy. "How do we stop them?"

"What do you want me to do?"

"They can't find the spring."

"They're going to find it if it's right up there."

"Make them stop."

"You want me to shoot them?"

"That's what you do, isn't it?"

"Just because I'm in the Army doesn't mean I go around shooting people. I have to have a reason."

"They're going to destroy the environment!"

"If it looks like they're going to destroy the environment right now, I'll shoot them. Deal?"

Farther along, Nick and Nora saw something and started running. Harlan and Olivia followed as fast as they could. Now the thinning of the trees was more obvious. Soon there were enough gaps to make out that there was a space ahead. They also caught glimpses of an odd darkness on the ground, as if they were approaching a deep hole.

Nick and Nora came to a halt at the edge of some break in the landscape. Harlan took Olivia around to the right to get a look at this break. They had to stay back from the very edge of the cliff, back in the trees to avoid being seen, but there it was, big as life. Bigger, really.

A dozen or so meters down from their position was a lake that extended far out toward the horizon, smooth and black as ebony, broken only by a few widely spaced trees. These trees were unlike the jungle trees. They were spindly, very like palms. They grew from within the lake. The tops of the palms branched far out from the trunk, like roots in reverse. At the top, each tree sported tens of thousands of leaves, maybe more. The canopy over the lake merged with the trees on shore, creating an unbroken shield against the rays of Iota. Harlan saw how satellites were once again useless here.

The lake itself was roughly circular in shape. They were too far from the cliff edge to look down and see the shore directly beneath them. Looking around the circumference, it seemed as if the structure that supported the contorted mass of life everywhere else on this planet had collapsed, leaving the worms and beetles and whatever else to cascade in a haphazard fashion down to the inky pool below.

Olivia seemed fixed on the shoreline; Harlan focused on the lake itself. It was hard to tell if she was right, if it was a pool of petroleum. The surface was so still it could have been solid, though the presence of the trees belied that. Looking closer at the nearest part of the surface, Harlan saw bubbles. It really was a spring. He smiled despite himself.

"It's incredible," Olivia said.

"It's big," he admitted.

"Not the lake. Look at the shore over there." She pointed past Nick and Nora to the break between the jungle and the lake. "It looks like a geologic artifact, doesn't it?"

"Uh-huh. So it's not?"

"Look at the structure." Harlan had a momentary desire to drop into a father-daughter paradigm and scold her. Why couldn't she just explain what she was talking about? Instead, he did as he was told. The fall from the jungle floor to the lake's surface wasn't a straight vertical like you would expect with some hard stone like granite. It didn't stair-step down like a soft limestone or loose soil. It had a notched appearance. Harlan scrambled for a metaphor.

"It looks like... the inside of a nut."

"A nut?" she asked.

"As in nuts and bolts. The notches look like the threads

in a nut. Very regular. In and out as you go up from the lake to the jungle. It looks built."

"It's not built. It's *grown*."

Just when Harlan was certain that he knew everything this planet could throw at him, something else appeared to totally unnerve him.

"Alright, let me see if I've got this straight. You're saying the ground under us, under all of these things crawling around, the actual ground down there is... *alive?*"

Olivia nodded, once again betraying a smile with her eyes.

"And this is its mouth?" Harlan couldn't repress a shudder. He barely repressed a desire to run flat out back to Bouyain Village, back to the shuttle bay, back to Gandhi.

"No. I think this is a wound."

That sounded even worse. "What wounded it?"

"The pressure from beneath... or... What if it's a pore?"

"Like on my face? A pore?"

"Why not?" Harlan kept one eye on Nick and Nora while Olivia continued to theorize. They were into their packs, working on something. He couldn't tell exactly what. "For hundreds of years people used a spiritual myth called Gaia to describe the Earth as a single living being. That's absurd, of course, even though it was a valuable tool for describing the interconnectedness of ecosystems. But imagine a world that truly is *alive*. What we've seen and catalogued here are merely the fleas and ticks on the hide of a giant beast. Out of the stuff that made this planet two billion years ago didn't come an ecosystem, but a life! A single, globe-spanning life that supports a symbiotic collection of lesser beings above and houses a furnace of molten, glowing rock below."

Harlan looked at her.

"You really believe that?"

"Of course I don't. It's a theory. It's actually a very bold theory, one that I intend to prove. I've been skirting around the edges of this for years now, but I didn't understand the significance of what I was seeing. Maybe it's not one creature, but a colony of continent sized beings, similar to tectonic—" Olivia stopped speaking when Harlan pulled out his gun. "What are you doing?"

"Remember what I said I'd do if they were about to destroy the environment right now?"

"Yes."

Harlan pointed to Nick and Nora. They were tinkering with a metal cylinder that stood about waist-high. Its silver shine made it stand out in the shifting tableau of gray on gray.

"That's a bomb," he said. Olivia's eyes slid past Harlan to the menacing device.

"You're wrong. What would energy scouts need with a bomb?" she asked.

"They're not energy scouts. Stay here, stay hidden." Harlan started moving toward the bomb. Olivia grabbed his arm.

"You're not going anywhere until you tell me what's going on!"

He rounded on her, the romance paradigm gone, the father-daughter paradigm forgotten. He was a soldier now, talking to a scientist.

"Why do you think they sent someone of my rank and experience to go on a hike in the woods? Nobody wants to drill for oil here, or if they do, I don't know about it, and I don't care. Those are terrorists, probably from Europe. They want to make a big statement, and blowing up that lake of oil would be a great way to do it. Thanks to you and your research, they've found it. Now I'm going to stop them. Is that all right with you?"

He turned away without waiting for her response.

Nick was still assembling the bomb. Nora was nowhere to be seen. She must have disappeared into the jungle while Harlan was lecturing Olivia. Harlan scanned the shoreline, and as far into the trees as he could see. He swore to himself silently and approached Nick anyway. Angling around behind the big man was easy. He was too intent on his bomb. Harlan was, for the first time, thankful for the sky full of buzzing creatures, the floor covered in skittering bugs. He had no trouble sneaking up on Nick, getting a bit more than an arm's length away. He lowered the gun and pointed at Nick's head, ready to shoot. A voice came from the jungle. It was a woman's voice. It wasn't Olivia.

"Harlan!" Nick spun around, goggling at Harlan. His expression, what was visible of it through the mask, changed to one of triumph. He even advanced, using his bulk as a goad. He wanted to provoke a fight, it seemed. Harlan scowled at him, gun still raised, and answered over his shoulder. "What?"

"You shoot him, I shoot the girl," Nora said.

On this entire trip, Harlan hadn't had to make any tough choices. He didn't enjoy trudging through the scary landscape, he didn't enjoy being lectured to by a fussy know-it-all, he didn't enjoy spying on terrorists or trying to foil their plans. But all of these things were part of his job, part of who he was, and the decision to send Harlan on this mission was someone else's. Now, though, he had a decision of his own to make. He didn't dwell on it too long; he didn't have the time. But his thought process was careful, nonetheless. He weighed his options and came to his conclusion.

"You've got a deal," he answered and slammed the butt of his pistol into Nick's facemask. It was a gutsy move, but he was betting that Nora would be so stunned she wouldn't kill Olivia immediately. And he was betting that she would realize her position was far from certain without a hostage. There was no sound of a gunshot, only a surprised grunt from Nick, and a thud as he fell to the ground, unconscious. The gamble had paid off.

Nora's voice shook with anger as she called from the jungle. "That was stupid, Harlan! Now, walk away from the bomb, toward my voice. And drop the gun."

"Yes on one, no on two." He moved into the trees, following her voice as best he could.

"Drop the gun or I'll kill Olivia, right now!"

Harlan was impressed. Nora was smart enough to use Olivia's name, instead of "the girl" or some other impersonal description. But he wanted to rattle her.

"I see you're new at this terrorist thing. Let me explain

something in plain language for you." He thought he was getting closer to the sound of her voice. "If you kill her, then I'll hunt you down and kill you. I'm good at that. Believe me. If you don't kill her, on the other hand, we can negotiate."

"Negotiation is worthless."

"Only if you consider your life worthless." He veered a little to the right, less sure where the woman was. "How do I even know you have Olivia? Have her say something."

There was a murmur of talk that Harlan couldn't understand, but it gave him more to go on for direction. The murmuring grew louder, escalating into Nora yelling, "Say something!" Silence followed, then a loud crack and another voice yelping in pain. Harlan recognized it as Olivia.

"That was a mistake," he taunted. And it was. Not because he was overly worried about Olivia, because he had Nora's position now, or at least a sense of it in his mind. He did a quick circle around, careful to make as little noise as possible.

"Where are you?" she called. Harlan didn't answer. He could see them now. Nora was standing, holding a pistol very similar to Harlan's. It was pointed at Olivia, who was sitting on the ground, nursing her head. She looked like she'd be okay. Harlan leaned against a tree, waited for an annoyed boa-cobra to slither out of the way, then braced himself to shoot, taking a bead on Nora's midsection, the surest way to get a hit, and not a bad way to get a kill. Then he noticed what was in her left hand, dangling at her side. She was holding something black, plastic: a detonator.

Could he get a headshot, killing her instantly? Doubtful. Could he shoot the detonator itself? Maybe, but also doubtful, and probably not advisable. He had no idea yet what the configuration of the bomb was. He was sure it was incendiary, not nuclear, which was some small comfort. But an accidental detonation would still be devastating, particularly to himself and Olivia at this distance. He couldn't risk that. So he had to try the direct approach. He walked out from behind the tree, not masking the sound of his footsteps now. Olivia looked up first, but Nora heard him soon enough. Harlan kept the gun trained on Nora.

"Drop the gun," she said, "and we can all walk out of here to a safe distance before I detonate."

"If you drop your gun, I won't kill you."

Nora actually started laughing. Olivia made a small gesture with her fingers for Harlan's benefit, as if to say, "Shoot her." He shook his head very slightly. Olivia frowned. Nora lifted the detonator, brandishing it like a weapon. Olivia watched the detonator carefully. Harlan was worried she was going to try to attack Nora, to take the detonator away. She would more likely get herself killed.

"I don't even need this. It's on a timer."

"How long?" Harlan used the question to distract Nora from his step forward. It seemed to work. Nora just kept shaking the boxy plastic device at him.

"It doesn't matter! I will gladly give my life for—" Nora never finished the sentence.

Harlan noticed a slight forward movement from Olivia. She was looking past Nora, through the trees. Harlan spared a glance that way. One of the Frisbee-ring creatures was flying toward Nora, toward the detonator in particular. Nora looked, too, but not fast enough to drop her hand out of the way.

The Frisbee ringed her hand, drawn by the strange smell of plastic. In a heartbeat, it contracted around her wrist, severing her hand from her arm with a metallic snap. The Frisbee's outer edge flared up and over both the hand and the detonator, enveloping them. Tiny wings that had been invisible in flight served as makeshift teeth, tearing into flesh and plastic as the whole bloody mess fell to the jungle floor with a wet thud like a piece of rotten fruit.

Nora, too stunned to realize that she was losing a dangerous amount of blood from her wrist, turned the gun on the Frisbee and shot it several times, destroying the creature, and what was left of her hand and the detonator. Harlan didn't wait this time. He put two rounds into her midsection, knocking her to the ground. He calmly walked over and put another bullet in her head.

It took him a moment to remember that Olivia was still there, sitting on the ground. Harlan dropped his gun and knelt next to her, oblivious to the myriad creatures around him, many of which were already feasting on Nora's corpse. He gave Olivia a hug. Her arm exploded.

Harlan looked up to see Nick, red faced with rage. His hood was off, the goggles dangling, broken and useless. With one hand he held his oxygen mask to his mouth. With the other he held the smoking gun on Harlan.

"You're helping me out of here before the bomb goes off."

"Like shit!" Harlan yelled, fear for Olivia finally making all of this personal. He almost went for his pistol but Nick shook his head.

"I'll shoot her again."

"I believe you."

"Harlan," Olivia said. He turned to her, still holding her. She was bleeding badly. He needed to staunch the flow and cover the wound immediately. "The bomb."

"I know."

"It'll destroy the planet."

"What?"

"Quiet!" Nick advanced. "We're leaving her here and going back to the village." One of the butterflies floated down from the tops of the trees and settled on Nick's left cheek. The wings of this one were angular, distinctive. Both wings together, when fully extended, formed an almost perfect five-pointed star. It was quite beautiful. Without thinking, Harlan started to warn Nick.

"Don't—"

"Don't let it bite you," Olivia interrupted.

Nick took her at her word, and slapped at the butterfly, smashing it into gray goo, which he then wiped on his chest. In moments, another butterfly landed on his chest and bit him through his suit. He screamed, destroying it as well. Three more attacked his stained hand. Five landed on his face. He kept trying to kill them, but there were too many, and the pain was clearly excruciating. Seconds later, he was covered in flapping, biting stars. Harlan and Olivia turned away then, waiting for the frenzy to finish.

The screams ended. A little later, the other sounds ended, too. They looked up. Nick and Nora's remains lay side by side, only their gray jumpsuits and a few bits of bone left. A butterfly floated coyly towards Olivia. Harlan clamped his hand over the wound on her upper arm. Olivia gasped in pain but said nothing. The butterfly became confused. It flew a lazy circle around the two of them, almost landed on Harlan's gloved hand, and then returned to the leaves above with its brethren.

"Are you okay?" Harlan asked.

"Just bandage me. We have to get to the bomb."

✧

"Where is it?" she asked. They were at the cliff. Nick and Nora's packs were lying right there. "Where is it?"

"I think it fell over the edge," Harlan said.

"Or he pushed it. We have to go down there."

"Look, Olivia, I know that you want to maintain the environment, but we don't know how long the timer is set for, we don't have any equipment, we—"

"I wasn't being melodramatic before. It *will* destroy the entire planet. We have to stop that bomb!"

"How? How can one conventional explosive destroy an entire planet?"

"The oil, Harlan, the oil. There's a pool of it down there, but it's also a major component in every living thing on this planet, and if the crust is also alive, which I think it is, then it's suffused with oil, too. One detonation, especially one near a lake like this, could cause a chain reaction that would envelop all of Africa, possibly crack open the crust, unleash the pressurized magma underneath and cause a planetary explosion that would rain debris all over the Iota System."

Olivia took a breath.

"You know this?"

"No! I don't! It would be difficult to prove experimentally, but it's a risk we need to avoid if at all possible! Don't you agree?"

Harlan took a tentative step toward the edge and looked over. All he saw below was a calm, black surface.

"Okay."

○

"What do you see?"

"Not much. I can't tell how deep the lake is. The bomb might be—"

"No, what do you see next to you? What does the wall look like?"

Part of Harlan was sure that if Olivia wasn't injured she would have offered to climb down the rope—which Nick had conveniently left in his pack—and she would have searched for the bomb herself. He was almost sorry for her, since she wasn't able to see what Harlan was seeing. Another part of Harlan wanted to smack her.

"The notch-out levels are solid, crumbly, kind of like a good New York cheesecake."

"What?"

"Sorry. It's like tightly packed sand, but softer, not gritty."

"What about the notch-in levels?"

"They're odd. You can tell this thing is alive on those levels. Hang on a second." Harlan lowered himself a little to get a look at the next level of the cliff face. "Okay, everything is still Africa Gray. This level looks... it looks like the inside of a mushroom, really."

"It does?" Olivia was very excited. "Let me drop a camera..."

"No. I've got enough to deal with down here as it is. I'll describe it, alright? There're rows of vertical... filaments, I guess, nearly two meters top to bottom. All very regular. Closer to the lake, a lot of them are broken, but they must be pretty strong because the broken ones are still standing straight up, like stalagmites."

"Stalagmites?"

"A feature in caves. Never mind. Farther in, the filaments are mostly intact. They're close-packed in their rows, but the rows are probably spaced about a half-meter apart. It's like they're the walls of tunnels into the thing."

"Harlan, do you think—"

"No. I'm getting the bomb and I'm coming up. The tour is over."

Hand under hand for two more minutes, and Harlan was at the surface of the oil lake. He looked out toward the palms. From this height, the far shore wasn't even visible. And there was still nothing to break the stillness of the pool other than an occasional few bubbles. Harlan found that eerie. He expected waves at least, but the wind here was minimal, not enough to disturb the heavy liquid.

"I still can't see the bottom. This stuff is totally opaque. I've got no idea how far down I'll have to go to find the bomb, but I've still got about five meters of rope. Would you check the knot on the tree for me? I'm going to be a lot heavier coming back up."

"Okay." Harlan waited, passing the time by etching his name into the soft cliff face. He got to the second "a" before he remembered it was alive. He was torn between erasing what he'd written and not wanting to touch it at all. "The line is secure," Olivia called down.

"Thanks. I'll be back."

Harlan lowered himself into the oil. He was surprised that it was so cold. He shouldn't have been. It seemed odd for oil to be cold, for some reason. It was also quite thick. He had to wait for his body to settle before he could get the next handhold on the rope. As the oil passed over his waist, he was aware that his legs were very hard to move. He was not going to have much freedom down there. Up over his chest. He was reluctant, for some reason, to let his arms go into the lake until the last possible moment. Up to his neck. He paused, moving his head around, taking one last check that his oxygen supply was securely fastened.

He dropped completely into the lake. All light was gone. All sound was gone. Even his sense of touch was reduced to just the feel of his hands on the rope. His hand under hand rhythm was broken when he couldn't feel the rope below with this right hand. He didn't panic, but it was a tough moment until he realized he could put his right hand just below his left, which was clutching the rope desperately, and slide it down. The rope hadn't dropped straight down into the oil, of course. It had floated near the surface. Harlan had to force the rope down with him.

He was a good two meters down when he started to doubt that this would work. He only had another three meters of rope left, and there was no indication that the bottom was near.

It was then that Harlan started to wonder if anything lived *in* the lake. Images of vicious eels, stinging manta rays, more exotic creatures that shunned the light of day bounced around in his head. He fought to control them, since they were only in his imagination, but that made them more numerous. They were all waiting, just out of reach, to attack. At any moment he would be enveloped in glistening skin, razor sharp teeth, skeletal limbs...

He felt something brush his shin and he screamed into the oil. He felt the bubbles roll up his face, which felt like something attacking his head. He grasped the rope tight and shut his eyes, fully aware that it was a pointless gesture in the dark. After a moment to collect himself, he felt out with his leg again. There was something there. Something solid. Something smooth and metallic. The bomb. He'd reached bottom.

Harlan let go of the rope. It was slow, but he knew the lake floor was just below him. He fell farther. Something was wrong. He reached for the rope, his arms slowed by the thick oil, and continued to fall deeper into the lake. He caught hold of something, not the rope, not the bomb. It was the edge of the cliff, one of the notch-out levels. He held onto it with both hands and stopped his fall. Slowly, carefully, he pulled himself up onto the ledge where the bomb had come to rest. He sat, legs dangling over an unknown drop.

Feeling around, he found the bomb and the rope.

Wrapped around Harlan's torso was another piece of

equipment that they had found in Nick's things. Nylon straps held a powerful electromagnet on his back. This was how Nick had been carrying the bomb, along with his other supplies. Harlan backed up to the bomb, which had landed upright on the shelf. He pressed a button; with a sharp tug and a noticeable thrum of power, the magnet connected. The bomb was now attached to Harlan's back. All he had to do was climb back up.

A whisper of movement in the oil surprised him. He dismissed it as his imagination and started to climb. Hand over hand, he pulled himself up, very slowly. The bomb was heavy; he was heavy. And the oil didn't seem to want to let him go.

He felt something brush past him again, along his left side, past the bomb. This time it felt very real. He climbed faster.

Another swish on his right. This motion was faster, urgent. As much as he wanted to, he was unable to climb any faster. He only had a meter to go and he would be out of the lake.

Something grabbed at him, pulled him backwards. He couldn't feel it touching his suit, so it must have been something in the dark, grasping at the bomb. In the back of his mind, he wondered if the magnet was attracting it... them. He yanked upward, and whatever it was slipped free.

He felt a pressure on his right. It was large. It was smooth. He couldn't tell if it was the size of a shark or a giant squid, but he wasn't interested in finding out. He kicked in that direction and the pressure shifted away. But he swore he actually *heard* the creature growl.

Feather-soft fingers started playing around his head, over his face and neck. He shook them off...

And then he broke the surface. The thick oil dripped off his hood in sheets. He was able to see a little. He kept pulling upward. Unseen things below were churning up the oil around him. He focused on the rope. By the time his chest was out, he noticed a noise from above. It was Olivia.

"Hurry! Climb faster!"

Harlan didn't like the sound of that. Up and up he went.

As his feet left the lake, he caught a glimpse of a vaguely round shape below, but he didn't stop to investigate. He kept climbing the rope until he reached the top, where Olivia was finally able to give him a little help. Harlan dragged himself away from the edge, then turned off the electromagnet. The bomb clunked down to the rough surface at the edge of the cliff. None of the jungle animals were foolish enough to come this close to the edge. He reached around for the controls and turned off the timer. He didn't even bother to look at the display to see how close they'd come. He sat up and looked out over the lake.

Harlan cocked his head, surprised. There were ripples in the lake. Big ones, quite a way out. They moved slowly toward the shore, but there was nothing to indicate what made them.

"What's that?" he asked. Olivia looked at him, wide eyed.

"It was coming this way."

Harlan got a chill.

"It? One thing? Did you see it?"

Olivia nodded.

"What was it?"

She leaned forward, as if to confide something, then paused.

"Do you really want to know?"

Harlan shook his head.

# VISIT

Europe

August 11-15, 42
*(May 4-8, 2313)*

"Father, promise you'll be nice."

"I'll be nice. I'll be nice."

Juliette knew her father too well; that's why she didn't trust him. Martin Burke did not bottle up his feelings very tightly, and even though she was fifteen years old, with a year of college under her belt, Juliette knew he still saw her as a three-year-old. Barry was going to have a tough time making a good impression when it would look like he was stealing Martin's little girl.

But, after all, what boyfriend didn't have trouble with the girl's father?

"I really like Barry, and he really likes me. That's what's important, isn't it?"

Juliette listened to a second or two of silence on the radio before Father answered.

"How serious are you about this boy?"

"He's not a boy, Father. He's a man."

The grunt she heard on the other end told her all she needed to know.

"Put Mother on."

Juliette spent twenty minutes commiserating with her

mother about the situation. They made plans for how to handle the fateful first meeting, plans that Juliette knew would come to nothing. Barry and Father would meet, and they'd either get along or not. There was very little she could do about it.

✿

The tram left Copenhagen—where Juliette and Barry went to university—at nine in the morning. The ten-thousand-kilometer trip was delayed by a wind-blown rock fall at Hebert Pass, where the tramline passed over the Equatorial Mountains. They didn't arrive in Berlin until well after noon.

Juliette spent the entire trip preparing Barry for his meeting with her father. All of that went out the window in the first few seconds. Barry carried their bags off the tram into the Berlin station where the Burkes waited. Barry walked right up to Juliette's father, towering over the shorter man, shot out a hand and said, "Good to meet you, Mr. Burke."

The look on Father's face showed an uneasy combination of amusement and disgust.

"So. You're the boyfriend."

Barry faltered noticeably. Mother introduced herself and welcomed Barry to Berlin. Juliette glared at her father. He kissed her on the cheek, pretending she wasn't angry. During the drive out to the farm, Barry and Mother talked about the tram ride, about college, about a hundred things. Juliette and her father remained silent.

✿

"Calling someone 'Mister' is a sign of respect in Copenhagen!" Juliette yelled.

"Keep your voice down," Father muttered without looking up from his workbench.

"They can't hear us out—" Juliette's response was cut

short by the whine of Father's extruder. He was making a
new set of blades for the plough. Ten seconds of metallic
shrieking ended, and Father said:

"What was that?"

"I said they can't hear us out here. You gave Barry the
cold shoulder because of a cultural difference that he
couldn't have known about."

"He could have, he just didn't."

For some reason that Juliette never understood,
honorifics like 'mister' and 'madam' had fallen out of favor
on this side of Europe. The simple life of the farmer was
more than just the norm; it was a kind of religion out here.
Even within the city of Berlin, most people eschewed any
kind of hierarchy, real or symbolic. This was one reason—
among many—that Juliette had felt the need to travel to the
far side of the planet for her higher education. She knew it
would be hard to maintain respect for her professors if she
wasn't supposed to think of them as more knowledgeable
than she was.

"Come in and talk to him. You'll like him."

"Your mother likes him. Isn't that good enough?"

"No."

Father turned to look at her. She was starting to notice
age taking its toll on him. His eyes were still piercing, but
shrouded in wrinkles. His hair was still thick, but the brown
was edged with gray now. The person who had, for the
better part of her life, embodied her concept of 'man' was
now middle-aged. Juliette's ideal had shifted to the kind of
man that Barry represented: tall, eloquent, graceful. He
would never excel at mending a tractor the way Father did.
Barry knew more about computers than combines. Where
Father's humor was colloquial, Barry's was urbane.

She wasn't really surprised that they didn't get along, but
she wanted to try to make it work anyway. It was
important.

Father gave in with a submissive tilt of his head and they
donned masks for the walk back to the house.

When they entered, Barry stood, always the gentleman.
Father waved at him to sit back down.

"I think he was standing for Juliette," Mother offered.

"Oh," Father said. "So, Barry, you're a tall one."

"I spent five years at school on Gandhi."

Juliette bit her lower lip as she took a seat at the kitchen table. This wasn't the way she wanted her father to learn that Barry had gone to private school on one of the moons of Asia. His opinion of Barry as an effete snob was becoming more entrenched by the minute.

"Gandhi, huh? Ran out of desks at the school in Copenhagen, is that it?"

Barry answered the barb with a friendly smile. "My parents have contacts with the Sakaguchi Corporation, and they heard about a boarding school that—"

"I see," Father said.

He pulled himself a glass of water from the purifier and took a seat at the table next to Mother. Barry sat down again, facing off against him.

"Look, Mr. Burke—"

Father tensed up.

"I told you to call him Martin," Juliette breathed.

"Fine. Martin. I love Europe. It's my home. But it's not the only place in the system. I'm glad I got a chance to see another culture, meet people from other worlds. You must understand that. After all, you sent Juliette to Copenhagen."

A small squeak of the chair leg rubbing against the floor said volumes about the change in Father's attitude. He leaned forward a little, just enough for Juliette to notice.

"I'm not sure I follow you there, Barry. What is it that I understand?"

"You have to admit that Juliette has benefited from her time away from home."

"Because she met you?"

"Martin!" Mother scolded.

"That's right," Juliette said, warming to the challenge. "Because I met Barry."

"Don't sell yourself short, hon," Barry said to Juliette. Father's temper jumped another degree upon hearing that nickname. "You're going to excel at whatever career you choose."

Juliette and her mother turned to watch Martin Burke's reaction to that. His face grew quite red. From anger, perhaps? From embarrassment? Or fear?

"I'm sorry," Barry said, his bravado quickly deflated. "What did I say?"

"I need to—" Father stood and left the kitchen in a rush.

Mother stood to go after him. Juliette put a hand on her mother's arm.

✿

He was back at the extruder, programming another plough blade, when Juliette came into the workshop. She pulled off her mask, mentally preparing the tirade she wanted so much to throw at him. He asked too much of her. He really did.

"It's your life," he said quietly, tinkering idly with the tool making machine.

"What?"

"If you don't want to take on... I suppose it was dumb to assume..."

"Father—" He fired up the extruder, drowning her out. She reached over and shut the thing off. "You thought I would take over the family business."

"There's a reason they call it a family business," he said, his head lowered. He refused to meet her eyes. She knew it was to hide the tears. She allowed him the failed deception. Truthfully, she never knew that the farm was so important to him.

"You wish you had a son."

Father pretended to sneeze, giving him an opportunity to wipe his eyes, then he faced Juliette.

"That's not true. Don't ever think that."

"Do you really think it would be worse for you to regret my gender than my life choices? I have no control over my sex. If that's all this was, it would be easier, don't you see that?" Juliette lost control right at the end of that speech and started crying. Father stood there for half a second, at a loss with a woman crying in front of him, but he rallied.

"Oh, sweetie." He took Juliette into his arms, for the moment just a strong father comforting his weepy daughter. "I know that a boy would want to leave about as much as you did." Despite herself, this made her laugh a little.

"Show me," he said. She shook her head, confused. "I know you've got his ring there somewhere. Let's see if this Barry character at least has a little taste."

Juliette fished in a pocket and pulled out a jewelry case. She handed it to her father. He opened it to find an engagement ring with a flawless one-karat quartz in a glowing bronze setting.

"That's quite a stone you've got there."

"I told him it was too much." Juliette, now that she could wear the ring openly, found herself mesmerized once again by the flashing brilliance of the expensive jewel. She enjoyed the weight of it on her finger. She knew that the history books said that engagement rings were a symbol of the husband buying the wife, but she didn't care. All it symbolized to her was how much Barry and she loved each other.

"Europe to Juliette." She looked up at Father, embarrassed by the way she'd fallen into a near trance.

"I'm sorry," she said.

"About what?" He looked at her quizzically.

"About all of it... I'm sorry you're disappointed."

"Well, I won't tell you I'm not. I am. But that's not the point. I don't want you to be disappointed."

She grasped his arm, tight, to make sure he heard what she was going to say. "I won't."

He nodded, then walked with her across the yard to the house.

# WINTER

Asian Moons

December 34, 75 – January 1, 76
*(June 19-25, 2357)*

Thank you for your query requesting either a statement or an interview. Since I am unable to respond to all such inquiries, I have attached a copy of my memoir of the events leading up to January 1, 76. I hope this meets your needs.

I formally waive all rights to this document and provide it to the public domain.

Best Wishes,
Helena Cochran

(Note: This version was last updated on March 3, 77 to correct minor errors in chronology and for style.)

**Anton Labrack,** the Council Member representing Europe, called me on December 34th. At the time, I was polishing a draft of his speech for the system's 75th anniversary celebration. I was on his yacht, orbiting Fuji. The Councillor was down on Fuji, the little submoon of Azuka, attending a conference; he contacted me during a break. As one of three senior aides to Councillor Labrack, I was not surprised to get a call from him, but the substance was unusual. He asked me to poll the other members of the Council on a proposal that he was drafting for the meeting on the 39$^{th}$. Even more unusual, he asked me to poll them in person. I agreed, of course. When I asked if he still needed me to finish his speech, he said he would take care of it.

My first task was to determine the location of all the Council Members. A quick net search showed that, as expected, all seven (including my employer) were on the moons and submoons of Asia, making a variety of public appearances during this last week before the anniversary. Councillor Labrack had earlier confided in me that there was a reason the celebration had been scheduled here around Asia instead of on the surface of Europe where the original landing occurred, but he did not explain further.

I signaled for the yacht crew to shut down the grav-chamber. As pleasant as the sensation was, I wouldn't be able to stay in the little pod. I had to arrange transport to Azuka, where I would be able to meet with three of the Councillors, though ironically not with Councillor Lyerly, the representative of Azuka itself. The yacht had to remain behind for Councillor Labrack's use. The chamber spun down and I lost the comforting illusion of gravity. Three white-suited crewmen escorted me from the grav-chamber to my quarters, and I arranged with them for the transfer of my baggage to a skiff that would take me to Azuka.

The trip from the orbit of Fuji to the surface of Azuka took eight hours in the skiff, so I took the time to review my notes on the Councillor's proposal.

The original concept of the Iotan Council was that each planet would be represented by one member. The populations of Azuka and Gandhi, the major moons of Asia, fought this, claiming that their varying needs required separate representation. A referendum was put to the system and narrowly passed, creating an amendment to the Iotan Constitution. Each of the moons was given one Council seat. (As a side note, I would add that in the seventy-seven year history of the system, the two moons of Asia only voted differently on three proposals, and those votes were all within the first decade of the Council.)

In the years since, other moons around the Iota System developed their own societies and economies, particularly DeGaulle, a moon of Europe, and Washington, America's only moon. There was pressure from both to repeat the referendum that gave the moons of Asia special dispensation. The proposal that Councillor Labrack was bringing to the Council was designed not to offer more exceptions, but to modify the basic membership requirements. Rather than have a planetary requirement with two (or more) exceptions, he instead drafted a population requirement of five thousand citizens for any body in the system. This would allow DeGaulle and Washington to send Councillors to Gandhi. It would also give status to Fuji and Ganges, the only two populated submoons in the Asian system.

It was hoped that the Asian Councillors would see this as a benefit.

☼

The landing on Azuka was smooth. I was instantly met by a driver who took my bags and led me from the gate. The gravity on the moon was quite a bit less than I was used to on Europe, so walking through the shuttle port was tiring. Timing my strides as I bounded through the concourse took more concentration and control than I had to spare after my long trip. We went past the entrance to the passenger train that ran from the port to Central City as it was pulling away from the station.

My driver, a tall lad who couldn't have been more than thirteen, escorted me down a hallway lit brightly by Asia, giving everything a strange greenish tinge. Dozens of clear, soft-sided umbilicals branched from the glass corridor to vehicles waiting outside the station. He found the appropriate door and keyed his entry code. I could see the car through the windows: a 75 CruiseMaster, a favorite of the nouveau-riche on Azuka. I preferred the ride of the six-wheeled Emperor, but the CruiseMaster would do fine.

The driver carried my bags through the airlock first, then showed me my seat. Disconnection from the building took only moments and we sped past the train toward the city.

Central City is the most prized settlement on Azuka because it is very rarely in any kind of shadow. For thirteen days it is lit by Iota, with only a brief six-hour eclipse behind Asia. For thirteen days it basks in the reflected glow of Asia. In the early days of colonization, it was hoped that Azuka would be the breadbasket of the system, but few harvestable plants could survive in the constant light on the Asiaward hemisphere. Fewer still could survive the thirteen-day nights on the far side. Farming was a bust on Azuka, as well as all the other moons of Asia. That was when the Azukans turned to electronics.

The gravity of Azuka is slightly more than half that of Europe, and the gravity on Fuji is significantly less, making for ideal conditions to experiment with and build electronic equipment that rivaled anything in the system. The preemies with knowledge of computers and engineering flocked to Azuka. Fortunes were built and industries created. Almost every programmable component around Iota was manufactured on either Azuka or Fuji.

There had been rumors in the zines for months that Sakaguchi Corporation, one of the leaders in transportation technology, was working on some sort of levitation device, and last week Yasuko Sakaguchi announced that the rumors were true. I hoped to catch up with one of the Council Members at a tour of the Sakaguchi research facility.

The tour was almost over when I arrived, so I snuck in quietly, staying in the back. A blank-faced scientist was droning about something or other, but the attention of the twenty or so visitors was focused on the demonstration behind the plexiglas wall. In the spacious clean room, something was happening that looked like magic; a platform the size and weight of a small car hovered a meter off the floor. It seemed quite stable, despite the fact that a heavy fission generator was attached to the far edge of the platform. Technicians, dressed head-to-toe in white paper clothes, moved around the thing, taking measurements and making notes. One climbed on a step ladder and stepped onto the platform, causing it to bobble only slightly. The technician made some adjustments to the reactor and the platform slowly descended.

"Are there any questions?" the scientist giving the tour asked. I knew who would be the first to speak up.

"How much does that thing cost?" Drew Kunz asked. She was the Council Member from America, and her loud, nasal voice woke up the room.

"This was a prototype, so the costs associated with it are not—"

"That's not what I mean, sonny. How much to get it flying like that?" Councillor Kunz had never had any trouble speaking her mind, plainly and bluntly. "Fission isn't cheap, you know."

"No, ma'am. I believe the reactor is generating approximately a hundred megawatts-per-hour."

"I only know a thing or two about physics, but I know plenty about economics, and that little contraption is going to have to get a lot cheaper before you're going to get anywhere with it."

That caused the room to break into murmuring. The scientist tried to regain control.

"I assure you, Councillor, we are continuously looking for cost savings. As I said, this is merely a prototype, so I think it's rash to jump to—"

Kunz's eyes flashed. She was not used to being lectured. "I'm not jumping anywhere, sonny. I'm telling you the God's Honest Truth. And another thing, if you're going to give lectures to tourists, you can say anything you damn well please, but we're not tourists, alright? So, the next time you get some real people in here asking real questions, why don't you go back to getting coffee for the *real* scientists and send us out someone who knows that there's no such thing as a megawatt-per-hour."

The scientist was silenced, so Kunz added, "I believe the tour is concluded. Thank you for your time." Under her breath, I heard her mutter, "Freakin' dildo." The scientist scampered out of the room as the crowd broke into conversation pockets. I recognized most of the faces: the cream of Azuka society, a handful of politicians, and Kunz's staff. She was commenting to one of her aides to make a note to review American research on levitation when I caught her eye. She smiled.

"Helena, what are you doing here?" She bounced over to me, even more awkward in the gravity than I. Native Americans top out around a meter and half in height, and Drew Kunz was a good ten centimeters shy of that, if you didn't count her gigantic mass of red hair. She gave me a hug and a peck on the cheek.

"Is Anton here?"

"No, Ma'am. He's still on Fuji. He asked me to come ask you a question."

"That's a long way to come to ask a question. I'll bet it's a doozy."

"I'm actually polling the entire Council. It's—"

"Are you? Well, I'm gonna make your job a little easier. You eaten lunch yet?"

✿

*Taste* is the most trendy and exclusive restaurant on the moon of Azuka. Somehow the owner had convinced the Central City engineers to allow a tower to be built *through* the city's dome. Coming up the glass elevator was an experience. Rising through a hundred-fifty meters, the whole of the city was laid out for our inspection: the central dormitory, nowadays housing for the lower classes of workers, the rows of labs and workshops which were mostly company owned, the ring of residences nestled inside the edge of the dome, once the neighborhoods of the rich and powerful, now home to the bourgeoisie.

Then, without warning, the city disappeared from view, replaced by a silvery dome. We continued another fifty meters to the top of the tower. The area immediately outside the dome was dry, arid, cold. A few scrubby plants were starting to make their way in the feeble atmosphere, though no animals could survive in it yet. Dotting the landscape were a handful of small domes, toy replicas of the city itself. That was where the real power lay, in those insulated gardens, maintained at incredible cost for the enjoyment of the top rung of Azuka society. Sometimes I wonder where the rich will go when the middle class can afford personal domes.

The elevator car entered the top floor. Councillor Kunz led me through the foyer, past the host, who didn't have time to greet us before the rounds began. As always, Kunz glad-handed everyone in the place on the way to our table: nods for the people she didn't like, waves for the people she tolerated, handshakes for the people she trusted, and occasional hugs for the people she truly cared for. I felt honored to have made the cut. We finally made it to the table, where Cecilia Matson and Beata Abrahamson were waiting.

"What'd you say, Cecilia? Not much, I'll bet!" Kunz gave the Antarctican Councillor a hug. Matson was kind enough to bend over, since she was quite tall and clearly didn't enjoy the ritual. Her smile was genuine, though.

"How are you, Drew?" she asked.

"Good, good. Beata? You look divine!" Kunz embraced the African Council Member, who was dressed in a bright orange suit that was at odds with the grays and blacks worn by the other diners at *Taste*.

"I feel so... out of place," she confided to us.

"Don't you worry about it! If I had your figure, I'd be wearing a pink dress with a saffron bow! You both know Helena, don't you? Of course you do. Sit down, sit down, everyone!"

Since I was the guest here, I waited for the Councillors to do their catching up, which was mostly about husbands and children and home upkeep. My job didn't leave me time for any of the three, so I smiled and nodded when it seemed appropriate. Kunz did most of the talking, but Abrahamson twittered for a while about some sculptor who was making a big splash on Africa. Matson said little.

"Cecilia," Kunz said, "you fly halfway across the system, and you've got no news?"

"There's nothing to report."

"Report? C'mon! You have a boyfriend yet?"

"No, I don't."

"A girlfriend, then?"

"No."

"What do you do for fun out there on Antarctica? Have snowball fights?" Kunz was always her own best audience, and she laughed at that one for what seemed like forever. Finally, she steered the conversation back to me.

"Well, Anton has another mysterious proposal that he's asked Helena here to run past us, so go to it, girl."

I outlined the proposal, trying to sound as much like Councillor Labrack as I could, appealing to our communal sense of propriety and fair play, citing the Council's history of similar choices, doing it all with reserve and dispassion.

"Well, that clever little bastard!" Kunz said. Abrahamson giggled at the phrase. Matson pursed her lips.

"I don't know what you mean," I said. "It's a straightforward proposal."

"There is no way in hell that Callahan and Lyerly would ever let that one go through."

"Why?" Abrahamson asked, not afraid to look a little lost.

I didn't understand, either. I said, "There would be extra votes for DeGaulle and Washington, but they would be balanced by two votes for Fuji and Ganges."

For the last decade or so, the Council had been consistently divided. Callahan and Lyerly voted as a block for Asia. Francis Bearden, the representative from Australia, was forced to vote with them, since Asia was the biggest market for the small planet's only industry: mining. There was always the implied threat that if Australia didn't toe the line then a serious effort to mine Asia's smaller moons would begin, and the Australian economy would collapse.

Africa was also part of the Asian coalition, but for reasons of security. Dozens of terrorist incidents aimed at the African biosphere had been thwarted over the last fifty years by the Iotan Army, which was trained, based, and commanded from Gandhi. The military now kept a constant perimeter around the fragile planet, and Africa returned the favor with its political voice. Beata Abrahamson was a friend and confidant to Kunz, but she would never vote against Callahan in open Council.

"You're right," Kunz said, "the votes would still be in Callahan's favor, but look at it another way. Right now, she can win any vote four-to-three. She's got a fourteen percent margin. You're asking her to drop it to six-to-five. That's only nine percent."

"They'd still win any vote," Abrahamson said. "I mean, we would." She blushed.

Kunz was about to answer, but instead, she glared at Matson, daring her to speak up.

"Capra," the quiet woman said.

"Capra's a small moon," I said. "We don't have any major settlements there. I think the population is only about two hundred."

"For now," Matson said. She sipped her tea.

"You change the rules like this, you can do all kinds of things," Kunz said. "You've got enough people on Europe, way more than Asia has."

"But we wouldn't just relocate people. It would—"

"Son of a bitch!" Kunz yelled. Several of the other guests at the restaurant looked over. Councillor Kunz didn't care. "That's what Anton is doing! It's brilliant!"

Abrahamson and I looked over at Matson, but now she was as confused as we were and shook her head.

"Look. Anton sends you out to talk to all of us personally. That means he wants this proposal to get some fairly wide attention before he brings it to Council. Why?" Kunz didn't give us time to answer. "Because he knows it will fail and he wants to put pressure on Callahan to deliver a compromise. Opening up the Council would be very popular on Europe and America, even if it doesn't mean we'd get a majority voting block. Callahan won't go for it, so she'll propose an alternate solution: a Lower Council."

I thought about that. I had read in school that the United States back on Earth had a two-house legislature. (Maybe they still have; I don't know.) Each had different responsibilities, but laws required passage through both. The Upper House (the Senate) was made up of two representatives from each State. The membership of the Lower House (for some reason simply called the House) was based on *population*.

"You're saying that Callahan might propose a Lower Council that would reflect population size?" I asked.

"Oh, she'll spin it as this great boon to Democracy, but she and Lyerly will strip it of any real power. That's what your boss is doing. It'll go over great with his constituency. Europe holds nearly a third of the population of Iota, doesn't it?"

"Yes," I said. This was a blow. What had seemed like a real chance for change in the Council, not big change, but something close to parity against Asia, had turned into a stunt for voters. If Kunz was right.

"Oh my," Abrahamson said. "This wouldn't be good for Africa. We've only got a few thousand people."

Kunz turned to her. "Don't worry about it, dearie. The Lower Council won't be able to *do* anything. It'll be a showpiece, focused on trivial issues like transportation safety and communication logistics. Maybe someday a hundred years from now, it'll rise up like the House of Commons did in Great Britain, but for now, your seat on the Council is far more powerful. Well, it would be if you could vote for yourself."

Abrahamson was confused. "Great Britain?"

✧

Gandhi, Asia's larger moon, was on the other side of the planet when I left Azuka. I couldn't get a better ship for the crossing. The intermoon shuttles were all long since booked up for the anniversary, so I rode it out in the same skiff... for twenty hours.

I was actually headed for Ganges, the submoon of Gandhi. Councillor Labrack's proposal would give Ganges full Council representation, but now it seemed that would never happen. It was difficult to accept that I was being used by Labrack. I was one of the volunteers on his original campaign three years earlier, and was happy to take a position on his staff. I had turned my back on a teaching job, among other things, to make this commitment, and I had done a good job. Some of Labrack's most popular quotes came from speeches I had written. No one outside government circles knew that. People always assume that politicians write their own words, or even that they think of them spontaneously. I was always content to stay in the background, but I knew that at least he understood my contribution, and I always thought he appreciated it.

But now, what? I was out of the loop, running a pointless errand to help him get reelected. I wouldn't have minded if I had known what it was for, but to keep me in the dark seemed pointless and hurtful. Thinking back, it had been a while since he and I had spent any real time together. I didn't harbor any kind of schoolgirl crush on him; I was too old and too cynical for that. But I did enjoy our time together, and anniversary planning had eaten into that time. So here I was on a tiny skiff without even the comfort of a grav-chamber, spending the most exciting week in the history of Iota making it clear to the six most powerful people in the system that I was a messenger for Anton Labrack and nothing more.

These were the things I thought about on that long trip, and when I finally reached Ganges, I was tired and in a bad mood. This is not the state you want to be in when meeting with Erik Lyerly.

Councillor Callahan kept a residence on Ganges, a palatial home under its own dome far from the military testing grounds and secret research labs that dot the landscape on the far side of the submoon. Iota shone bright on the golden dome as the skiff came down to the private landing port.

Councillor Lyerly was staying there temporarily while

the anniversary celebration approached. I was shown to the main office by a steward who announced my presence through heavy, curlicued doors.

"The Councillor will see you now," the steward said. I tried to smile at him, then went into the office.

I have to admit that I have no patience with spectacle. That's what this office was: pure spectacle. The ceilings were twice as high as even native Gangeans would need, the walk to the desk took nearly ten seconds, even in the very low gravity, and the desk itself was carved out of a huge slab of dark marble that could only have come from Australia. All of this was designed to make me feel small. It didn't work.

Erik Lyerly is a powerful, tall man, almost two-and-a-half meters, with dark hair and eyes. There is a menace behind his gaze that he doesn't often hide. It is a tribute to the Azuka political machinery that this man could be elected to represent that moon. Stories were told of his connection with Georgia Callahan, that he was her lackey, her hatchet man, perhaps her lover. I believed the first two without question. I chose not to dwell on the third.

My preexisting dislike for Lyerly, disappointment with Councillor Labrack, and fatigue from a long journey put me into a mood, so I started things off very poorly. As Lyerly started to rise from his chair to greet me, I addressed myself to the other man in the room first.

"Councillor Bearden. Good to see you." Francis Bearden was visibly stunned by the faux pas I had made. He stood to the side, behind the still seated Lyerly, blinking through thick glasses. He didn't quite stutter his response.

"Helena, always a pleasure." He glanced over at Lyerly, who was seething.

"Councillor Lyerly, I hope you're well," I said. Lyerly nodded to me, not rising. Without waiting for an offer, I sat in one of the plush chairs facing the desk. It made Bearden seem out of place, standing like a servant, but there was nothing I could do about it.

"I have been asked by Council Member Labrack to bring a proposal to the two of you for your thoughts. It deals with—"

"I know what it deals with, Helena," Lyerly said. "I don't let people take my time unless I know what they are trying to do with it. You can go back to Anton and tell him that it won't work."

Bearden was starting to sweat. He ran a hand over his thinning hair.

"So," I said, "you're saying you are opposed to changing the rules for membership on the Council."

"Labrack doesn't want to change the Council. Weren't you listening to Kunz? He wants to create a Lower Council." Lyerly's eyes flashed. I realized that he must have heard about my meeting at *Taste* and forced Abrahamson to talk. Neither Kunz nor Matson would have crumbled like this. It was a surprise, but I didn't see a need to back down.

"Would you oppose that?" I asked. Lyerly didn't answer, so I looked to Bearden.

"I think—" Bearden started. Lyerly raised a hand to stop him.

"Nobody here cares what you think, Francis. You think what I tell you to think."

I felt my face getting flushed with anger.

"That's uncalled for!" I said. "He is a Council Member, after all." I didn't even like Councillor Bearden that well. He was a weak man in a weak position, but unlike Beata Abrahamson, he didn't seem to mind. It was foolish of me to stick up for him.

Now Lyerly stood, towering over both of us. "The needs of Australia are closely tied to the needs of Asia—or didn't you know that?"

I stood as well, though I still had to look up to confront this bully.

"Of course I know it, just like I know that Africa relies on you for its security, so it is forced to ally with you as well."

"Africa requires security because of *European* terrorists," he said. "Or am I misinformed?"

That took a little of my bravado away. He was right. Most of the people calling for terraforming Africa were agricultural workers on Europe, working in harsh conditions on an unfinished planet of our own. Creation of a stable European atmosphere was hampered by savage biannual storms during each conjunction with Asia. We were playing a two-steps-forward/one-step-back game with our biosphere, and it was taking its toll on the average farmer, who still had to produce more each year despite the fact that until the terraforming was complete, the food industry was closely regulated. The population around Iota had exploded in just seventy-five years to nearly half a million. They all needed food, which only Europe could provide in quantity.

The radicals said that Europe should play a more forceful role in system politics. The extremists said that politics was a waste of time and had tried to attack Africa themselves, always with dire consequences.

"Europe is a difficult place to live and work," I said. "You know that. We have over a hundred fifty thousand citizens. We are the breadbasket for the entire system. Why shouldn't we have more power?"

Lyerly walked around the desk to confront me personally.

"Do you know what this Saturday is?"

"Of course I do. It's the seventy-fifth anniversary of the Europe landing." I couldn't help putting a little emphasis on the word *Europe*.

"Do you know what's significant about seventy-five years?"

"It took *Hermione* seventy-five years to get here. That's why we're doing something special for this New Year's celebration."

Lyerly smirked a little. "*Hermione* flew here in seventy-five *Earth* years. Why should we celebrate after seventy-five *Europe* years? Do you know how many Earth years it has been since we landed?"

I shook my head. Bearden piped up. "About a hundred."

"That's right. What happens on Earth a hundred years after a colony ship lands?"

Again, I was lost. My frustration at being a step behind

was giving me a headache. Lyerly kept his glare on me, but said, "Francis?"

"According to the original Stellar Charter," Bearden said, "if the colony is still viable after one hundred years, Earth will send a resupply mission."

I felt a shiver run up my spine. I looked back up at Lyerly.

"Kunz almost had it when she said that the Lower Council would take over communications logistics," he purred. "Labrack planned to use this proposal get a Lower Council, and to use the Lower Council to take control of the beam to Earth."

Another layer was revealed, and I didn't know whether to be proud of my employer or even angrier at my ever-widening distance from the truth. Nobody around Iota really cared what information we sent to Earth. The place was as remote as Valhalla in most people's minds, including my own. We all accepted that the Council had control over the information flow through the beam, and that Asia had control over the Council. The days when information from Earth was of great value were long gone, along with all the preemies. It had never occurred to me that they might be censoring the information flow *to* Earth, whitewashing it to make the situation here rosier than it really was, downplaying the discontent that was brewing in the system.

"The resupply mission is scheduled to depart in less than a year. A hundred thousand new preemies are going to be headed our way. Personally, I don't want half of them to be soldiers." He leaned down very close to me. "Do you?"

✧

I had only one more visit to make: Georgia Callahan, Council Member representing the moon of Gandhi, the defacto leader of the Iota System. She had at her fingertips the political power of Gandhi's capital city of Bombay, the technological wherewithal of Azuka, and the combined might of the Iotan Army. The longest standing Council

97

Member, she had originally been elected to her post fifteen years earlier, taking a situation that was already in Asia's favor and locking it down with steely precision.

What made Callahan such a difficult political opponent was that she seemed to share none of her comrades' faults. She was vocal, charming, strong, self-assured, restrained, and above all, approachable. She was neither evil nor maniacal, so she wasn't like some classic villain of literature. She had single-mindedly shaped the power structure of Iota to benefit Asians at the expense of everyone else, and that was why I opposed her.

It was the morning before the council meeting when the skiff landed, so I called her office from the port to make an appointment. One of her assistants set up the meeting.

☼

It is impossible to maintain a stoic cynicism in the children's wing of a hospital. I could feel a lump in my throat and wetness in my eyes as I watched Georgia Callahan read a book of nursery rhymes to ten dying children. Was the catch in her voice just as real, I wondered? I don't know, but I hated her for being so damn likeable when I wanted to throw this whole terrible week in her face. When she finished and the children said in unison, "Thank you, Councillor Callahan," I actually let out a half-sob. It was embarrassing.

Callahan caught my eye as she said goodbye to the children, and I followed her out into the hall.

"It's really a shame that we can't do more for these children," she said, looking back through the glass wall as the children went to their beds for a nap.

"I'm sure they're doing everything they can," I said. Why was I consoling this woman?

"We've been on the beam to Earth, trying to see if there's anything we can do, but they're as stumped as we are." She was rubbing it in. She knew why I was here, she knew the implications, and the implications of the implications, and she was teasing me. I wanted to scream at her, but I couldn't, not during naptime.

"Well," she said, turning to me. "I understand you have a proposal from Anton that you'd like to run past me." She was going to make me go through the routine, pretend I didn't know she had the whole thing all figured out. This was the most degrading moment of my life, but I didn't back down from it. I stormed ahead.

"Ma'am, the Councillor would like to propose a change in the membership requirement for the Council. Instead of one representative per planet, with an exception for yourself and Councillor Lyerly, he is proposing to allow any body in the system with five thousand or more citizens to have a Council Member."

She tilted her head, as if surprised by the notion. She hummed to herself for a moment.

"I like that idea. I agree."

I stood silent for five seconds.

"Helena?" she asked.

"Yes?" I responded.

"Are you alright?"

"Yes... I'm just tired. Thank you for your time, Councillor."

She smiled a winning smile at me.

✿

Councillor Labrack arrived in his yacht that evening. I met with him in his hotel room for five minutes and told him the substance of my discussions with the other Council Members. At my description of Drew Kunz's outburst, he nodded. His response to Erik Lyerly's pronouncements was to clear his throat. Only Callahan's comments prompted him to speak. He said, "Hm."

He was deeply distracted, but I was too angry to care. I showed myself out as soon as I could.

✿

The Council Chamber sits on the top floor of the Bombay dormitory on Gandhi. It is one of the oldest buildings around Iota. The Chamber itself is a study in preemie thinking. The ceiling is too low, only three meters, claustrophobic for natives of any of the smaller moons. The walls are coated by some odd sort of plaster, a disorienting tan color, and not built to last. It needs touch ups between each of the biannual Council meetings. Dominating the room is the Council Table, a circular monstrosity that was carved out of actual wood, brought from Earth. The hideous brown thing is inlaid on its surface with a trite quote from some long ago Earth politician: "One for all and all for one." Around the table are the Council Chairs, each made of wood with brass fittings, and upholstered with a material made to resemble the cured hides of animals.

Walking into the Chamber felt like walking into the Middle Ages.

My consolation was that the aides to the Council Members sat at the edge of the room in much more comfortable chairs. I sat behind Anton Labrack as the session came to order.

Seated on the far side of the table, facing me, were Callahan and Lyerly, with Abrahamson to the left and Bearden to the right. Kunz and Matson flanked Labrack. The sides were clearly drawn.

"Ladies and Gentlemen of the Council," Labrack started, "I would like to make a proposal for discussion and vote. Do I have your leave?" All the heads around the table nodded. There was some obscure rule in the constitution that required these niceties. "Thank you. I would propose to revoke Amendment III of our constitution and to simultaneously apply a new, XVIth Amendment, which would alter the membership of the Council in the following way. Each body—"

"Anton," Callahan interrupted. "I think we're all well aware of your proposal. I suggest we waive the formal reading and move directly to discussion." Again, heads nodded. Callahan looked to Lyerly.

"There is no need for change," Lyerly said. "All people around Iota are represented on this Council fairly and equitably. We have wisely kept modifications of our constitution to a minimum. This Amendment would be frivolous."

"Frivolous, my ass," Kunz said. "Seven people governing a system of a hundred thousand makes a little bit of sense, but we're up to half a million and growing. We need diversity." She was already laying the groundwork for a Lower Council. Did she know that Lyerly was prepared for that?

"Diversity is not in itself a worthy goal," Lyerly said. He seemed to be holding back, not going for the throat like he normally would. Something seemed off.

"Diversity leads to widened understanding," Labrack said.

"An interesting point, Anton," Callahan said. "You're implying that the Council lacks understanding?"

"As individuals, we all lack understanding," Matson said.

"Take it to the next step, then," Lyerly said. "Make this a true Democracy, with each citizen voting on every proposal."

"A true Democracy can never function," Labrack said, "but neither can a Dictatorship."

"This is not a Dictatorship," Callahan said, leaning forward slightly. Labrack had pushed a button there.

"It's close," Kunz said.

Labrack held up a hand and said, "There is no need to get contentious. My point is merely that at the two extremes of governance theory lie Dictatorship and Democracy, and neither have historically been successful. A happy medium exists somewhere between. I simply propose that we slide closer to Democracy with an expanded Council and reap the benefits of a more multifaceted point of view."

"All you want—" Lyerly said, getting ready to pounce before Callahan stopped him.

"I think this discussion has been very fruitful. I suggest we vote." This seemed strange to everyone in the room, even Lyerly, who was straining at his leash. Labrack had proposed nullifying one Amendment and ratifying another. The bare few minutes of talk didn't do the subject justice.

"I would like to make one minor suggestion, though, before we commence," Callahan said. Silence in the room. "You proposed making the population limit for entry into the Council five thousand people. That seems... restrictive. I would like to lower the number to fifty."

"Fifty? Are you serious?" Kunz asked.

"Yes."

Lyerly seemed to figure out his ally's ploy. He started to chuckle to himself. No one else seemed in on the joke.

"You realize, Georgia," Labrack said, "that our moon of Capra currently holds a population of over two hundred?"

"Does it? Excellent. That's the sort of small community that gets lost in the shuffle of this Council. I look forward to meeting whoever Capra sends to Gandhi. I'll begin. Yea."

Beata Abrahamson, who hadn't said a word so far, seemed pleased to add her "Yea."

Kunz was about to vote when Labrack leaned over to her, whispering. "What?" she asked loudly.

"Just do it," Labrack hissed. He sensed the same thing I did, that the Asians had something up their sleeves more devastating that a mere bluff. Callahan wasn't the kind of politician who bluffed.

"Nay," Kunz said, with a defeated tone. Callahan smiled. Lyerly sneered. Bearden seemed about to keel over from tension.

"Nay," Labrack said, making a small bit of history. Never before had a Council Member voted against one of his or her own proposals. He looked to Matson, who nodded.

"Nay," Matson said.

I was watching Lyerly and Callahan enjoy their triumph, though I still didn't understand it when I heard Bearden say:

"Nay."

"What?" Lyerly growled.

"I'm voting against this proposal. Nay."

"You should rethink your vote, Francis," Lyerly said. Callahan put a hand on his arm, but Lyerly shook it off. "This proposal is in the best interests of the system."

"But not my planet. It'll be ruined."

"Ruined?" Kunz asked.

"The Asian moons," he stuttered, facing Callahan. "You'll populate them all. That's eight more votes for Asia on the Council on top of the two for Fuji and Ganges. Asia will dominate the Council. But the only way to make settlements on those moons profitable is to start mining. Australia's economy will be in ruins in a year. I can't let that happen!"

I looked at Callahan, furious with her for manipulating us, but still impressed by her gamesmanship. Labrack's schemes were like orbits within orbits, and instead of trying to sneak a deeper scheme into the mix, she knocked the whole system out of alignment by altering a single number.

Lyerly glowered at Bearden, his face getting red. "I should throw you off of this goddamn building!"

"You just try it, big boy," Kunz threatened, standing from her chair.

Lyerly stood as well, his huge height putting his face into shadow under the low ceiling.

"Enough!" Labrack yelled. Everyone looked to him. Lyerly and Kunz sat. "The proposal is defeated, the status quo retained. You still have your Council, Georgia."

"It's not my—"

"Yes! Yes it is!" I was stunned to hear the Councillor so emotional. The hurt in his voice tugged at me. "It's your Council. You control it completely, and I wasn't able to make a single dent in that control." He paused. "Does anyone even care what I was really trying to do?" He waited, looking from face to face. I had known the man for three years, and had never seen him look so defeated.

"I do," I said, surprised I had spoken. Labrack turned in his chair, and the smile on his face broke my heart.

"Thank you, Helena. I'll tell you. I didn't want to expand the Council, or build a Lower Council, or take control of the beam to subvert the resupply mission from

Earth. All I wanted was to remove the pricing restrictions on food."

"You can't do that," Abrahamson said, horrified.

"I know, Beata. As I just learned. But it is the best way, the only way to give Europe's economy the boost it needs to calm the extremist elements that are so intent on destroying *your* world."

"Oh," Abrahamson said, suddenly embarrassed.

"Anton," Callahan said, "you know that it would be disastrous to the entire system if food prices weren't capped. You're growing the only food we have. Next you'll suggest we deregulate the water from Antarctica."

"Yes, I would," Labrack said. "You can sell your electronics and your ships for anything you want. We have created the most lopsided economy in history."

"A person can live without a car or a computer. They can't live without food or water. There is no reason you can't start your own industries. Look at America. They're already producing shuttles on Washington." Callahan looked to Kunz for confirmation.

"And the Gandhi corporations are undercutting us, sometimes even selling at a loss, because they can afford to. You get your raw materials from Australia at a deep discount," Kunz said.

"They buy in bulk," Bearden said.

"They buy in bulk," Labrack said, "because they have the resources to do so. We do not. We are in a hole too deep to dig out of, and it is causing a strain on our entire populations. Europe's dissidents are the first to appear because our population is so large. The promise of an idyllic life, promised to us by our fathers and our grandfathers, is being blown away by devastating storms, harsh laws, and an economy stretched to the breaking point. Something has to give."

There was a moment of silence. Finally, Callahan continued the meeting. A few minor proposals were raised and debated, but everything after the discussion of Labrack's Amendment felt like an anticlimax. I walked with the Councillor out of the building, back to our hotel.

✿

The trip to the far side of Gandhi was coordinated by the Iotan Army. Fifty sub-orbital planes shuttled government dignitaries, corporate officials and members of the media to the remote site. A variety of live links with Bombay and the other major cities in the system would broadcast the proceedings to the general public. I tried to arrange not to sit next to the Councillor on the two-hour flight, but it couldn't be avoided.

Labrack was still stewing over his defeat, and I was still angry about his treatment of me. We sat in silence and watched the bleak landscape of Gandhi roll into shadow on the dark side of the moon. Somewhere near the terminator, he said, "Francis. That was my mistake."

"Excuse me, sir?"

"I should have told him what I was doing. I did not think he had the nerve to stand up to them."

"What are you talking about?" He seemed to remember I was there.

"I'm sorry, Helena. I was just thinking out loud."

"I know. Why would you have let Bearden in on your plan? Didn't he save it from disaster?"

"What? Oh, no. I wanted the modified proposal to pass."

I shook my head. Another reversal was not what I needed just then.

"I know I treated you badly," he said. "I was playing everyone. This proposal on its face was frivolous; Erik was right. DeGaulle does not need its own representation—at least not yet. I sent you out to start people talking, trying to guess my motives, build some paranoia in the Asian camp. It worked. I was truly stunned by Erik's conclusion about my motives. I should have thought of the beam to Earth. But I suppose it is too late to work that angle now."

"I'm confused, Councillor. You *wanted* Callahan to lower the population limit?"

"Yes. I want eight more Asian moons with

representation on the Council. It would be perfect."

"Perfect for what?"

"I was serious when I said that my major goal is to deregulate food prices. I only hope my performance wasn't too over the top."

Performance. Even the impassioned speech in Council was an act. I didn't know anything about this man.

"With all those mining colonies voting," Labrack continued, "it would be easy to start by deregulating *metal* prices. Don't you see?"

"Eight mining colonies," I said, "along with Australia, would be more than enough to deregulate metal prices. And then you would have nine independent groups who wouldn't be beholden to Gandhi and Azuka."

"We could deregulate food and water. Francis doesn't even realize that he torpedoed a proposal that would have given his planet a huge amount of power in the system."

"He thinks the other mining operations would run him out of business. Those moons all have lower gravity, so extraction would be much less expensive."

"They would corner the market on the lighter metals, like aluminum, but Australia still has the only significant source around Iota of uranium."

"For fission," I said, everything finally clicking into place. It was a brilliant scheme. Labrack convinced Callahan to change his own proposal in such a way that it appeared she would gain... but she would eventually lose. He even had to make sure that his own coalition voted against it so that Callahan wouldn't be tipped off, or else she wouldn't actually populate the minor moons of Asia. And the whole precarious balance of the thing was tipped by Francis Bearden.

"He figured out what she was going to do. Unbelievable," Labrack said. "But now she has an idea of how to completely dominate the Council, and I'm sure she will try to find a way to make it work. We'll eventually get what we want."

He smiled at me. I couldn't smile back.

Soon enough, a light appeared on the horizon. As we

approached, it resolved into a landing strip, lights flashing in sequence, giving the pilot clear direction where to land. Nothing on the moon's surface was visible beyond the narrow airstrip. The touchdown was smooth, and we taxied off the strip to a parking lot to make room for the jets behind us. The first shock of the evening was the blast of cold air when the pilot opened the door. There was no umbilical.

"They have a breathable atmosphere?" I asked. I was handed a parka by a flight attendant as I left the plane. The stairway to the tarmac was skeletal, but solid. I pulled the coat tightly around me, feeling the warmth drain from my face and hands. The Councillor stepped down behind me and put a hand on my arm.

"What does it feel like?" he asked.

"It's cold."

"I mean breathing open air. I assume this is your first time."

I was stunned to realize it. It was the first time I had ever stood in the outdoors without an oxygen mask. We were among the first ever to do that in the entire history of Iota.

"They've come so far. Not even Azuka has this kind of atmosphere, and it's smaller than Gandhi."

"Gandhi needs a shield against Asia's radiation more desperately, since their orbit is closer in. Gandhi is going to be easier to terraform than Europe. But someday we'll get there."

A soldier in cold weather gear saluted the Councillor and escorted us to a car nearby. We bundled into the car, thankful for the warmth. The soldier drove us down a paved street. We could only see the few meters directly in front of the car. I assumed he knew where he was going.

Our destination stood in the dark like a dream, lit by powerful floodlights. It was just a box, possibly a warehouse, or a hangar. We were let out of the car next to the entrance, one pair of hundreds of guests that were trickling in from the airfield. Inside, the hangar was heated and warmly lit. Dozens of guests milled around the open space, passing from table to table where a variety of appetizers were laid out. Alcohol was flowing freely. As well planned as this all was, someone hadn't realized that the parkas wouldn't be needed in here. Some were still wearing theirs open. Others had dropped theirs on the floor near one wall. I kept mine handy, in case some new surprise was in store.

Councillor Kunz called me over to her group. She was drinking a dark concoction I didn't recognize and munching on an overfilled plate of food. She was at the center of ten women, all much taller than she, but she held court like a queen, regaling them with stories of her previous husbands. They weren't drunk yet, but they were working on it. They were laughing much too hard. I looked back at Labrack. He was talking with Callahan. I didn't like the look on his face. I excused myself to talk to him, but was sidelined by Francis Bearden.

"Have you heard, Helena?" That one sentence confirmed he had also been drinking heavily. I was concerned he might not survive the cold air when we had to leave.

"Have I heard what, Councillor?"

"The moons of Asia. They're going to let me mine them!" He was glowing with happiness.

"The Asians are allowing you to settle the moons yourself?" It seemed an odd choice for Callahan and Lyerly.

"Oh, no. That would be much too dangerous. I'll be doing it robototically."

"Robotically."

"Yes. No people, just machines. It's brilliant, don't you think?"

"That's wonderful, sir."

"We'll make a fortune!"

"I'm sure you will."

"I'm sure I will, too!"

"Excuse me, sir."

Labrack's dream of using the minor moons of Asia as the start to a bloodless revolution on the Council was gone now. Callahan had destroyed it and at the same time reinforced her alliance with Australia. I didn't know what the Councillor would do now.

I left Bearden and went to Labrack. I assumed he had heard the same news I had. He was trying to put on a brave face, but I could tell this was not an act. He was totally outmaneuvered. There was no way that Europe could get out from under Asia's thumb now, and he knew it. Callahan knew it. We all knew it. We would have to find a way to live with it, I supposed.

"Sir, I—"

Feedback from a poorly configured public address system whistled through the room, bringing all the conversations to a halt.

"Sorry about that," Callahan said over the system. "If you'll follow me to the amphitheatre, we'll get started."

Double doors slid open at the far end of the hangar, revealing a brightly lit stage and several hundred seats. The whole thing was surrounded by banks of lights raised up on poles, washing out the stars. The blast of chill air sent people running for their coats. A soldier motioned for the Councillor to follow him. He went up on the stage, where nine chairs waited. I stayed offstage with the other aides as the Council took their seats. I was only a few meters away, but for some reason, my attention was pulled toward the monitor to my right. It displayed the scene on the stage from the perspective of a camera somewhere out in the stadium. The look on Labrack's face was colder than the wind as he shook hands with the other Councillors.

The crowd in the stadium took their seats; Labrack went to the podium.

"Ladies and gentlemen here on Gandhi, those of you watching from the other worlds of this system, and those of you watching from Earth, I greet you. I am Anton Labrack, Council Member representing the planet Europe."

There was polite applause. I was surprised to hear this was being sent back to Earth. It was odd to think that people on Earth might see this before anyone on Antarctica.

"On December 5 of Earth Year 2182, a journey began. That journey brought one hundred thousand scientists, farmers, miners and explorers to this system. Our ancestors had a grand vision and made their vision a reality. I stand here under an open sky, breathing the air of Gandhi. This is a testament to their bravery and fortitude that makes me glad to say... I am an Iotan!"

The applause this time was more passionate. I felt that tug again deep inside, but I tried to ignore it.

"My remarks this evening will be..."

I looked up from the monitor to the stage. His speech ran, "My remarks this evening will be brief." I had written this portion of it. Lyerly noticed the pause as well, and called to his aide, an olive-skinned lad nearly as tall as his employer.

"I will save my remarks for later. I want to bring out the first two of our special guests this evening."

The aide took some sort of instructions from Lyerly and ran offstage again as I heard a commotion behind me. I turned around. Coming through the hangar was... was history.

We all saw why there were two extra chairs on the stage. They needed no introduction, so Labrack gave them none. Every child around Iota learned at a young age the names and faces of Lois and Clark, the android pilots who brought *Hermione* across fifty-six light years from Earth to Iota. Everyone in the arena stood. The surge of applause was huge, as if we could hear the rest of the system applauding with us. I couldn't help myself; I burst into tears.

The androids shook the hands of each of the Council Members, who had also stood. I think I actually saw a tear in Lyerly's eye at meeting these icons of our entire culture. They hadn't aged, of course, still the modestly handsome pair that helped found the original colony on Europe so long ago. I noticed that their parkas were different from ours, electrically heated, I assumed, because they don't generate any heat of their own like humans. They run on the ambient heat of their surroundings, to make it easy for them to work with humans in most settings. This setting, out in the cold night, was very different, and I expect frightening for them, but their smiles were real. We must all seem like children to them. Like *their* children.

With the greetings accomplished, Lois and Clark took their seats and Labrack continued.

"Twelve years ago, the last remaining preemie from Earth, a teacher named Elaine Yang, died on America. Now, the only living connection we have with our ancestral world sits on this stage... or perhaps not. We have one final guest for the evening."

The lights went out. A gasp came up from the crowd. The monitor next to me was still working, though. The camera tilted up to the sky, filled with stars now that the floods were off. The speaker system was also still working, as Labrack's voice filled the night.

"Ladies and gentlemen, may I present our last guest for the evening, *Hermione!*"

With precision I had not thought possible, at that exact moment a glow appeared in the sky, directly overhead. I ran out from the backstage area, along with the other aides and stage personnel, to look at it for myself. The glow was a blue dot at first, moving slowly but perceptibly against the seemingly fixed stars. Soon it grew into a blue trail in the sky, like a lens flare, or an artificial comet, or a harbinger of good fortune. Again the crowd roared, not in the slightest skeptical that what Labrack said was true. Somehow we all knew that what we were witnessing was the exhaust of the legendary ship, long since retired to a distant orbit of Asia, now brought into orbit around this moon for us to celebrate tonight.

The burn lasted for a minute, maybe more, but I wish it had been longer. For that minute, I wasn't worried about the machinations of the Council or my own disappointment with Labrack. I was in awe of what two androids and one ship had done so long ago.

The blue glow faded and the lights came up. The other aides and I scampered back out of sight as Labrack continued.

"It was seventy-five years ago tonight that Eliot Burke piloted a shuttle down from *Hermione* and brought the first humans to Europe, to begin a new life here in this system, for all of us. This was not the first extrasolar colony, and it certainly was not the last. But it is ours, and we imbue it with qualities of which we should all be proud.

"In preparing for this event, I did some research on Earth history."

Now Labrack was totally off the script. Lyerly made a gesture to his aide. The tall man nodded and left. I considered following him, but I wanted to hear what Labrack had to say.

"We know that the planets of this system were named for the continents of Earth, thanks to our friends here."

Lois and Clark shared an amused look that I didn't understand. I suppose that any couple who has been together for a hundred-and-fifty years will communicate in ways others can't fathom.

The monitor went dead. I looked around. There was another monitor on the other side of the stage. It was also dead. That's what the aide had done; he'd cut the feed out to the other planets. And to Earth. No one knew what Labrack was going to say, and it scared Lyerly enough to do this. It scared me, too.

"In Earth history," Labrack continued. "Asia was the largest continent and had the largest population. But it was Europe and America, younger societies, smaller societies, that dominated the planet's economy, government and culture for five hundred years. It is a supreme irony that, on Iota, the reverse is true."

The Council Members were stunned, none more so than Georgia Callahan. For the first time, Labrack was doing something she didn't expect and couldn't control. The signals coming from this arena were cut off, but there were two hundred people out there in the audience who would take his words back with them. Some were recording sensories for their personal use. Whatever happened here wasn't going to stop here. Callahan couldn't stop that.

"Asia, with their smaller population but superior financial resources, now runs this system. My planet, with one-third of the Iotan population, is relegated to nothing more than servitude as farmers for the rich. This has led to extremist elements, elements I have strived to control but cannot, who call for active response. Violent response." He paused. The crowd, the world, held its breath. Would he call for an escalation of violence? Deep in my heart I hoped he wouldn't, but by this point, I couldn't imagine what he was thinking.

"I cannot allow such a response." I almost heard the sigh of relief.

"One of Earth's best loved poets wrote the following: 'Now is the winter of our discontent.' That is where we are now, ladies and gentlemen. Europe is rife with discontent. Not because we have a hard life. Not because we are plagued with planetwide storms that destroy our settlements even as they destroy our crops, but because we are not given the freedom to make our own future.

"It is for this reason that I announce Europe's secession from the Federation of Iota."

Turmoil broke out in the crowd. Labrack walked off the stage, right to me. He was shaking, and not from the cold.

"What have I done? What have I done?"

"What you had to do," I told him. I didn't know if it was true, but that's what he needed to hear.

The podium remained empty while Callahan and her coalition talked. Matson and Kunz were also discussing something. At the far end of the stage, Lois and Clark were shocked and embarrassed to be on the same stage with this madness. Finally, Kunz went up to the podium. Her head barely reached the microphone, but her presence brought the room back to something close to quiet.

"Anton Labrack has done a rash and possibly foolish thing. But he's not going to do it alone. America also secedes."

More pandemonium as Kunz walked off the stage.

"I hope you know what you're doing," she said to Labrack.

"I don't," he admitted.

"That's okay, too," she said.

Callahan and Lyerly stared at Cecilia Matson, waiting for her response. If anyone else would leave the Council, it would be her, but if she did, it could be disastrous for the system. She finally stood and took the podium. Again, the room calmed down.

"Antarctica is the primary source of water for the Iota System. It would be cruelly unnecessary for us to break that lifeline with you." Callahan's response was obvious relief. "For that reason, we will maintain all existing water contracts with all bodies in the Iota System. Nonetheless, we secede from the Federation."

She walked over to us. Kunz gave her a big hug. Labrack shook her hand. We turned back to the stage.

"You can do it, Francis," Kunz urged under her breath.

"No," Labrack said. "They've given him too much. And Beata still needs them." He turned back to the two women. "We're on our own for now."

Callahan moved to the podium and spoke about stability and loyalty and hope for the future with her three allies at her side.

We left.

✧

I have not spoken with Anton Labrack since that day. He returned to Europe to help build a new government, one that could function apart from Asia. It was a difficult time for him, for all Europeans, and they're still working at it.

I left Gandhi and took refuge elsewhere. We were all targets, even the aides. No one believes that I wasn't privy to Labrack's intentions. I hope this memoir helps to set the record straight, though I doubt most people will believe it.

Anton Labrack is vilified in the remaining parts of the Federation, and remains a hero all over Europe and America. To me, he stands between these two extremes, a man on the cusp of history. And only history can decide whose view of him is right.

# WIDOWHOOD

Europe

*February 26, 77*
*(December 27, 2358)*

A crowd of over a hundred people huddled around the gravesite. The mourners were a mixed group of family, friends, neighbors and a few curious well-wishers from Berlin who braved the cold in somber clothes to pay their respects to the Burke Family.

Vera McCanliss stood by the gravestone in the windy, cold air. Temporary windbreaks planted at the head of the little valley deflected the worst of this year's storm away from the graveyard. The gusts that flapped at her black mourner's outfit and tugged at her oxygen mask were just eddies. She ignored the weather, as she ignored the preacher and his stock platitudes. She was only thirty-one years old. She was too young to be a widow.

The only thing that kept Vera from collapsing to the ground was the boy standing next to her, arm in her arm. Eliot wasn't yet thirteen. He was far too young to lose his father, and was still in a kind of shock. She needed to be strong for him.

The vagaries of genetics had ended the Burke Family in name, but not in legend. To commemorate the family's founder, Vera and Drake had named their firstborn Eliot, after his great-great-grandfather. Neither of them had the chance to meet Eliot Burke, who had died of radiation poisoning back in 29. Almost fifty years after his death, he remained an icon of Iotan history: the first man to set foot on Europe, but also a template for the ideal modern farmer. The Burke Family was not a dynasty of political power or monetary wealth, but of dirt and tireless labor. People all over Europe—and around Iota—grieved at the loss of two members of the Burke Family.

To Vera's left stood another new widow for whom the nobility of the farmer seemed to be merely a concept: Juliette Whitman, Vera's mother.

✹

The old farmhouse still sat under a low hill on the Berlin Plateau. The metal walls that fronted the place had been harvested from the container of a nearby drop of supplies from seventy-six years ago. A fresh coat of pre-oxidized silver made the place look new again. The windows, though clean, were yellowing with age from the harsh radiation of Iota.

Entering the home, one saw more space than expected. Excavations deep into the hillside had extended the house over the years. The furniture, those original iron pieces that remained, had been recycled—except for one chair that had been donated to the museum in Kiev. New aluminum furniture gave the rooms a contemporary, yet still homey feel.

Visitors filled the house. Fifty of those present at the interment followed Vera back home for the double wake for her father and her husband. She performed the strange dual role of bereaved wife and generous hostess. Vera had found wakes awkward as a child and ridiculous as a teenager. Now, living through one, she sensed the logic of it all. She was forced to listen to endless anecdotes about her father Barry and her husband Drake, but she didn't have the time to dwell on their passing and drop into a deep depression.

Vera watched her mother, Juliette, work the crowd. Juliette played the grieving widow as well, but she did it with more style and less humility. She accepted the kind words, and offered kind words in return. When someone mentioned her husband Barry's penchant for designer clothes, Juliette didn't shake her head sadly; she bubbled with laughter. She didn't seem nearly as sobered by her loss as was perhaps appropriate. Some of the guests threw sidelong glances at her, their disapproval clear. Maybe that was just the way they did things in Copenhagen.

As punch gave way to vodka, the wake got louder. No one took to dancing or singing, but the reminiscences veered from the staid—"Drake was such a loving father"— to the rowdy—"Barry never lost a game of racquetball, if you know what I mean"—to the downright apocryphal— "You know, Barry tried to buy Drake off to keep him away from Vera." And on and on it went.

Vera let the words wash over her the same way she let the wind whip past her at the cemetery: unheeded.

Finally, their bellies full and their consciences clear, the guests began to disperse. Eliot retreated to his room and his endless radio chats with friends in Berlin; Vera was left alone with Juliette. Vera knew Juliette blamed her for Barry's death. She wasn't looking forward to hearing all about it.

☼

Juliette Whitman was already the Grande Dame of Copenhagen before the birth of her first—and only—child in 46. She and Barry gave little Vera the best of everything that Iota had to offer. As a planetary sales rep for Sakaguchi Electronics, Barry's family wanted for nothing.

Back on the Berlin Plateau, Martin Burke continued to work the farm, usually employing local boys for a season or two. He kept in touch as best he could with his prodigal daughter. He didn't fit in well with the high society over on the eastern hemisphere, but he was a loving—perhaps doting—grandfather to Vera. Vera responded as granddaughters ought—she loved Martin unconditionally.

After Vera turned nine, she begged her parents to let her spend the storm season of 55 on the farm. They couldn't think of a way to talk her out of it, so off she went.

She only spent seven weeks on the farm, but it changed her life completely. The unvarnished affection from Martin stood in stark contrast to the genteel parenting Vera was used to. The work on the farm—Martin didn't allow an adolescent like Vera to skimp on her chores—was backbreaking and, at times, terrifying. The Storm of 55 was remembered as unusually brutal.

Helping out on the farm that year was Drake McCanliss. Drake's family owned another homestead to the south, on the slopes of Mt. Orange. Since Drake had five brothers, he wasn't crucial to their labor plans. It made more sense for him to earn some cash working for the Burkes.

For Drake, laying eyes on Vera was love at first sight. For Vera, the process took a bit longer. There were no cute, bantering fights; no dramatic life-or-death rescues; no protestations of affection that were disregarded one day and then gratefully accepted the next. What Vera did was develop a working relationship with this boy that turned into friendship.

On Vera's last day, Drake awkwardly pulled her aside and gave her a tentative kiss goodbye. Then he walked off and Vera left the farm thinking he was a sweet boy.

Ten minutes after she returned to Copenhagen, she sent Drake a radio message. Then she sent another two hours after that. By the end of that week, she realized that if she didn't see him again soon, she might just die.

No, Barry Whitman had never attempted bribery to end the relationship between his precious Vera and "that farmer lad". Barry was a loving and compassionate father, and understood exactly nothing about teenage girls. What's more, he knew he understood nothing about Vera, so he left the matter to Juliette.

Juliette understood the young female mind all too well. She tried to interest Vera in some of the more comely young men in Copenhagen. She nearly convinced Vera that Drake already had a girlfriend and he was keeping it from her. She spent two weeks complaining loudly that all men are troublesome, a plan of attack that Vera's father found moderately unnerving.

Juliette whined and cajoled and coerced. And it almost worked. Vera came to the brink of breaking off her relationship with Drake a dozen times, and a dozen times he had calmly and simply reassured her that they should be together.

Eventually, Drake proposed and Vera accepted. Martin, who had rejected a dozen very reasonable offers for his land, quickly altered his will to leave the farm to Vera. Juliette was far from worried about the loss of the inheritance, which had until then been bequeathed to her. What she was worried about was that Vera would be returning to a life of drudgery and despair on the family farm.

Vera and Drake were married in June. The happiest day of Vera's life was the saddest day of Juliette's, and for precisely the same reasons.

As the years had toughened Juliette, they had softened Barry. He visited Vera and Drake—and little Eliot—as often as possible, sometimes with Juliette, more often without. Before the end, Martin and Barry had finally become friends. Vera was overjoyed by that. Even Juliette had to admit she was pleased.

Barry continued to visit the young couple after Martin's passing in late 66. Juliette had tried, off and on, to keep her husband from traveling during storm season, but Barry was usually not persuaded. He certainly had no intention of missing Eliot's graduation from secondary school.

The ceremony, held inside the Berlin dome, went without a hitch. The tram ride back to the farm was windy but uneventful. Barry was scheduled to fly back to Copenhagen in the morning, so Drake only had the afternoon to show him the new moisturizers he had installed in the western fields. Barry wasn't any more

interested in farming that he had been when he first visited
the Burke place decades earlier, but a good gadget? That
always interested him.

No one ever determined if the accident occurred on the
ride out to the fields or on the ride back; the storm threw
the truck a hundred meters from the road, and the bodies
weren't recovered until they had long since frozen during
the night.

In a moment, Vera entered widowhood along with her
mother.

☼

"Vera, stop. Don't worry about it."

Vera looked up from the stack of dirty dishes to her
mother, who was sitting at the kitchen table.

"We don't have a maid, Mom."

Vera knew Juliette preferred to be called "Mother".
Vera reverted to "Mom" to needle her. It was an old trick.
Vera wasn't proud of her penchant for childishness, but she
did accept it.

"That's not what I mean. We need to talk."

Talking was precisely what Vera did not want to do. She
carried the dishes to the sink and started the hot water.

"Vera," Juliette said in her most commanding tone.

"Mom, I'm thirty-one years old. What makes you think
you can order me around like that? It's kind of sad."

When Juliette didn't shoot back an equally acerbic
comment, Vera turned around. Juliette was crying. Now
Vera felt even worse. She'd made her mother cry. She
turned off the water and wiped her hands.

If there was one tool that Juliette never used to get her
way, it was tears. She preferred to get her way through a
position of power, not weakness. Vera sat down next to her
mother and took her hand.

"I'm sorry."

"No, no, dear. You've lost a father and a husband. I
should be comforting you."

"You lost a husband, too. You and Dad were together forever."

Juliette let loose a hitching chuckle. "I suppose it seems like forever to you. It's gone by so fast... so fast."

How could thirty-five years of marriage not feel like forever? How could Juliette not understand what she'd had? She'd been with Barry for nearly three times as long as Vera had been with Drake.

Vera blinked. She'd been trying so hard to process the grief since the accident she hadn't completely processed the outcome of the accident. Drake was gone. It was such a little thing, really. Three words. Drake was gone. She'd never see him again. It was almost too strange a concept to imagine.

She'd miss her father, certainly, but how could she survive without Drake? He was a huge part of her life. She might just as easily ask how she could survive without her stomach or her liver. Even if she had lost a limb, she could replace it with a prosthesis. There is no such thing as a prosthesis for a missing spouse.

Unless she married again. Vera shoved that thought aside roughly. There was no way she would ever marry again. It hurt to even consider it.

"I envy you, dear."

Vera's head shot up. "You what?"

"You're young. You'll bounce back from this. I don't know if—"

Vera had to shake her head to deal with that. "I'll bounce back? What are you talking about? If you think I'm going to rustle up some new husband, you don't know what you're—"

"Vera, you have a son in the next room who loves you! That's what'll keep you going!"

"You have a daughter right here!"

"A daughter who resents me."

"Resents you?"

Juliette's weepy voice instantly turned to steel. "Don't tell me you didn't wish you'd grown up here in this house. Don't tell me you weren't looking for a way to get away from me. I know you better than that."

"Mother, I love it here. I always have, but I wasn't trying to get away from you."

Vera was lying, but only a little bit. What she said, it was mostly true. The revelation that she loved the farm was simply her coming to understand how she wanted to spend her life. It wasn't some sort of rebellion against her parents. At least, she didn't think it was.

"Mother, look... Why don't you stay here with me for a little while?"

Juliette shook her head.

"Why not?"

"Vera, this farm... killed your father." She whispered the idea, as if afraid to voice it loud enough for the farm to hear.

"No, Mother. The storm killed them."

"If it wasn't for this goddamn—"

"Mother!"

"—farm, they would have both been safe in a dome, in Berlin or in Copenhagen, or anywhere else!" Juliette jumped from her chair as she pounded on the table with her fist. Vera had no idea her mother resented the place so much. To Vera, this was home. She couldn't imagine living anywhere else.

"You don't know that," Vera chided.

"Come back to Copenhagen with me. Eliot would love it. He'd make new friends and—"

"We're staying here, Mother."

Some of the fire went out of Juliette's eyes. Vera thought she looked quite sad and lonely without it.

"We'll visit, though. After the storm season is over. Okay?"

Juliette nodded, and left the kitchen, silent.

# SUMMER

Australia

July 11, 63 – April 15, 80
*(December 26, 2340 – February 22, 2363)*

This is the story of Summer Kozlowski. She was
born on July 11, 63 to Ivan and Greta Kozlowski, extraction
specialists working in the uranium mines of Australia. The
happy couple, who never had any other children, were fond
of remarking that they named their daughter Summer not
because she was born during that traditional season, which
of course meant nothing to them, but because the little girl
brought warmth and sunshine into the cold and dark of
Australia.

The Kozlowskis taught Summer to be a lady, or as much
of one as was possible in the little mining dome of Darwin,
but they also taught her to be self-reliant, as she needed to
be during their long absences in the mines. Greta
maintained close contact with Summer during their stints
away from home through a company-provided radio relay,
but Summer had to learn at a very early age how to clean her
clothes and recycle her water and prepare the food packets
that the company sent to their dorm room each month.

When she reached the appropriate age, Summer went to
school with the other children in the dorm. Most of the
students lived lives very similar to Summer's, so she never

learned to resent her parents for their absence. She took it as a part of childhood like any other. It was at school that Summer met Gregor Tupov.

The boy, often called Greg by his gruff parents, was tall and dark and mysterious to Summer as only a boy can be to a girl of four. Gregor had two sisters, so girls were commonplace to him, and he ignored Summer's attentions for a very long time. She tried everything to spend time with him. She offered to help him with his studies. (He had trouble with Geology.) She offered to cook for him. (Only his sisters had been taught to keep house, and since they were recently married, Gregor was at a loss.) Gradually, Gregor understood that Summer was not just another girl to be treated with disdain like his imperious sisters, but a contemporary, someone who understood his life, perhaps even more than his rambunctious male friends.

In Second Grade, Summer asked Gregor to marry him. He punched Summer playfully and said yes. They went back to their computer game, fighting each other with interplanetary ships.

The lives of the miners on Australia were hard, but they weren't as dangerous as the Olden Days on Earth. Suffocation from landslides, burns from flameouts, respiratory failure from black lung, these things were unknown to the Australians. Most of the hard work was done by robots while the miners controlled operations from self-contained habitats either at the mine's mouth or nestled in some pocket deep under the ground. Shifts were three months in length, but the company gave bonuses to anyone who worked two shifts in a row. The Kozlowskis could not afford to stay out of work for long, and as a couple they could not stand being apart, so they worked six months on and three months off. Summer received only a third of their time in person, but they were careful to use it well and treated her with kindness and love.

Just after Summer turned eight, she, like most girls her age, had her first period. Her mother had prepared her for this, telling her what to expect and how to prepare. It was exciting and frightening for Summer, but her mother calmly talked her through it over the radio. Greta promised that she and Summer's father would be home in two days, after the shift ended.

Summer got the news during math class two days later that her parents had both died in a shuttle crash. Her excitement and fear were now laced with grief and sadness and anger. Gregor's parents took her to the funeral, which was a simple ceremony in the Orthodox tradition. The priest wore a tall hat and said that Greta and Ivan had gone to a bright, warm place far from the cares of Darwin. Summer knew nothing about God except that he was important and far away and she should ask him for help if she felt the need. That night, sleeping on the floor of the Tupovs' living room, she prayed to God to bring her parents back to her. She wept a little, then fell asleep.

She dreamed. It was unlike most of her dreams, which were about falling or flying or burrowing in the ground with her hands like a machine. This dream had a quiet, calm feeling, very real. She was walking across open ground, far away from the dome and the mines. But she could see just fine, which seemed oddly normal. Slowly, the light grew, and she could make out the ground in greater detail than she ever had before, each rock, each pebble crisp and clear in the light. Every object, including her own body, threw a distinct shadow. The shadows all went the same direction, backwards, away from where she was going.

On the horizon was a glow. That's why there were shadows. There was light on the horizon, widely spaced, as far to the left and right as she could see. But it was brightest directly ahead. Something was coming that excited and scared her. She heard her mother tell her it was alright. She heard her father tell her he was proud of her. And then the brightness swelled and filled the sky, bathing her in light and warmth. A song like angels singing filled her ears and she was so happy because she'd found where her parents went.

And she woke up. She lay on the floor in the dark of the room, nestled under two blankets and lying atop a third, listening to the air vents click and hum. She considered her dream and realized God hadn't given her back her parents, but he had shown her where they were. He had shown her Heaven. She smiled and fell back asleep. Afterwards, she never really remembered the dream, but she never really forgot it, either.

The Tupovs arranged for Summer to stay with Gregor's older sister, Ilena, who had married a doctor named Jinpeng Tang. The couple lived full-time in the dome and were happy to have Summer join their family.

As Summer grew into a young lady, she changed. Her interest in Gregor waned and then disappeared. She became a top student, acing any test that was about math or science, and doing well in other classes, too. By the time she was ten, all of her friends were very interested in boys, but she never had a similar interest. Sex was something she knew about, but not something she was interested in. Thinking about it was exciting, but it was also frightening, and it made her sad and angry, too.

Gregor started trying to spend time with Summer, making excuses to visit his sister, or asking Summer for help with his homework. She was always polite with him, but she made it clear that they could only be friends—distant friends, at that. Gregor tried to change her mind for a year, and Summer didn't understand why he was so insistent. There were many girls his age in Darwin, and most of them were much friendlier to Gregor than she. For a year he tried, then he gave up. Summer was quietly relieved. It gave her time to study.

Their class graduated from school in December of 75. Just after the ceremony, the news came from off-planet that something was happening. Three other planets, Europe, America and Antarctica, had all left the Federation. The reasons for this turmoil were discussed and analyzed by almost everyone in Darwin, but Summer found it tedious. She was more concerned about her job placement in the company. In early January, the assignments went out. Gregor was sent to Extraction, where Summer's parents had worked. Summer herself was assigned to Research and Development.

The R&D department was daunting for a young girl fresh out of school. Fifteen of the smartest people on the planet worked there. They treated Summer like a servant for six months before she forced her way onto a habitat redesign team. She bided her time, doing calculations and analysis for the senior staff, waiting for her opportunity.

In the design of any habitat, the least efficient process was heating. Much of it escaped into the thin, cold air of Australia, and it was expensive to produce, even though they kept the habitats at the bare edge of acceptable human conditions. In every mine was a smelting mini-factory that cooked the minerals and extracted the required metals with extremely high-temperature furnaces. For safety reasons, the smelters were always kept far away from the habitats, usually down in the mine near the extraction machines. So Summer drew up a system of connected ceramic pipes that could be run from the smelter to the habitat and back. When the pipes were filled with water, the furnace would quickly heat the water, turning it to steam, which would rise in the pipe and rush up toward the habitat. Most of the heat of the water would be lost to the perpetual Australian night sky, but some would also transfer into the nearby habitat, returning the steam to water, which would continue around the loop until it fell back into the mine to be reheated. For the cost of five kilometers of pipe and a few thousand liters of water, Summer had permanently increased the energy efficiency of the habitats.

No one treated her like a servant after that. She had her choice of projects, and she chose to work with a new material design that the company had recently licensed from the Sakaguchi Corporation. It was called a heat mirror. A nested collection of carbon pyramids, each only a few hundred molecules across, were layered one on the other. The layers were sandwiched between atom-thin sheets of a variety of metals: indium, platinum, lead, etc. The combination of the carbon and the metal sheets resulted in a fabric less than an inch thick that could reflect 99.9999% of any heat radiation or conduction.

The possibilities were astounding. Habitats wrapped in

this could reduce heat loss to their environment to almost nothing. Smelters coated with this material could attain their intense temperatures with only a fraction of the energy requirement. There were any number of ways that heat could be conserved with the heat mirror technology.

Summer came at it from a different perspective. She wondered what could be accomplished by *reflecting* the heat of your *environment*. Could you send a probe into the maw of a volcano? Could you protect workers as they maintained a still-working smelter? Could you mine Iota itself with vast heat-mirrored nets that flew through the seething upper reaches of the star at high speeds? This in particular intrigued her, since the star would be an excellent source of deuterium and tritium, which were so scarce on the planets of the system. She thought you could do all this and more. She started by building a pressure suit.

By April of 79, Summer had clearance for her first test of the heat mirror suit. It was a bold plan. She wanted to take a shuttle to the very edge of the nighttime hemisphere of Australia and then *walk to the dayside*. If the heat mirror technology functioned in such adverse conditions as well as it did in laboratory tests, she would be able to brave the hottest place on the planet, on any planet, with little or no discomfort.

It took longer to come up with a practical reason to even attempt such a thing, but she found it. After her graduation, the company had begun mining operations on the minor moons of Asia, which made the more expensive operations all over Australia less valuable, except for those specializing in the rarer elements, like plutonium and Darwin's specialty, uranium. Uranium was in high demand for the ever-increasing energy needs of the Iota System.

Uranium was difficult to extract and always laced inside larger pockets of gold, a worthless metal that was commonplace all over the system. With the suit, and some other special equipment that had yet to be built, Summer had found a way to mine uranium simply and cheaply.

The test was scheduled, but the company insisted that Summer be accompanied by another person, an extraction expert. She was stunned to find out that Gregor Tupov was going to be that expert. She couldn't believe that it was a coincidence, and learned that Gregor had volunteered after he heard that the project was hers. They had a civil reunion followed by a terse briefing. Then they went out on the shuttle to the edge of Australian night.

The suits were bulky, but no more uncomfortable than a space suit. The mirror fabric was a dark gray color, somewhat mottled, and it tended to sparkle in bright light. It was flexible enough, so movement wasn't a problem. The helmets were also made of the fabric, but reinforced with an interior of plastic to help them keep their shape. A face plate was out of the question, since it wouldn't be able to reflect Iota's heat and would boil the occupant through even just a square centimeter of plastic. Instead, a tungsten-iridium-cased camera was mounted on each suit's left shoulder, with a radio feed to a virtual screen on the inside of the helmet. Summer and Gregor practiced walking around with the slanted perspective that the camera provided for nearly an hour next to the shuttle. Summer could see the pilot laughing through the window. She waved to him.

Satisfied, they packed up their gear and started walking across the desolate landscape. Tiny lights mounted above each camera lit their way. They talked through a radio link. Summer described working in the R&D lab. Gregor talked about his job, too. They soon ran out of things to say, because Summer had no personal news to report, and Gregor did not seem interested in offering any news of his own.

They veered into politics as a last resort, and Gregor practically exploded with his anger about the treatment of Europe. He was very impressed with a man named Labrack who led that planet. Labrack knew what people wanted, and didn't care about giant corporations or government institutions. Summer didn't agree with a word Gregor said, but she was intrigued by his passion on the subject, so she kept asking questions.

Summer and Gregor were so involved in the

conversation that they didn't notice the glow on the horizon until it was quite prominent. They turned off their lights, and the rough, rocky land was still clearly visible on their screens. The Iota light was just creeping over the edge of the world toward them, throwing shadows from every rock back the way they had come. Summer felt an intense anticipation building, unlike any she ever remembered before. Gregor continued to talk, amazed by what they were seeing, but Summer remained quiet until Iota exploded over the horizon and filled the sky with hard, bright light. At the same time, an eerie whining, almost like voices, filled her headset. Gregor told her that it was interference from the radiation the star was throwing at them, distorting their radio communications. He had experienced similar phenomena in the mines near large deposits of radioactive minerals.

A small corner of Summer's viewscreen showed the ambient temperature of the air and the ground. It was climbing now, from the low of -220°C that they were used to on the night side of Australia. They needed to keep going until they got to a temperature of several hundred degrees.

Summer had never experienced the glow of Iota. She had spent her entire life on the constant night of the dark side of Australia. Other people, most people in the system, saw Iota often. Once a day, once a month, whatever the local cycle was. She had been told there were places where the sky was never dark, but she didn't believe it. She thought that constant light must make a person go mad. After only an hour walking through the Australian day, she was growing weary of the brightness. On the next trip, she would have to include controls in the suit for the helmet's screens, to turn down their intensity.

Gregor stopped to pick up a rock from the surface. The thermometer already read over 100°C. Water would boil here, Summer realized. She asked Gregor if he could feel any warmth from the rock. He said he couldn't. He tossed it towards Iota. They kept walking.

The ideas Summer had, for fleets of heat-mirrored mining cars swarming over the sizzling landscape, were grandiose, probably impractical, but Gregor listened to them and told her how proud he was to be part of this expedition, how proud he was of her. That made her heart flutter a little bit.

After two and a half hours of walking, they saw their first pool. It shimmered straight ahead, bouncing Iota's rays like a mirror. Summer ran to the pool. It was only a few centimeters across, but it was the first indication that her theory was right. She pulled a molecular scale from her belt and dipped the sensor end into the silvery pool. After a moment, the readout determined the average molecular weight of the sample: 65.39. Zinc. Melting point, 419°C. She checked her thermometer. The ground here was 450 degrees.

She was right. Ores that would lie buried meters under the ground on the night side were drawn to the surface by the combination of Iota's rays and the significant geothermal energy that this planet still carried from its earliest days of formation. Since Australia kept one face to Iota constantly, year after year, eon after eon, the heat in the planet's core was thrown into a chaotic turmoil in the crust, superheating everything in it. The tough minerals, mostly igneous in nature, stayed in a constant magmatic soup, but the metals were liquefied, boiled and forced into a gaseous state. Under such pressure, the metallic gas rushed through the magma, escaping through cracks in the cooler upper crust, finally seeping onto the surface where they returned to a liquid form and collected to bask under Iota in crevices and craters.

Pools, streams, lakes of zinc, magnesium, copper must have dotted the entire hemisphere. At least, that was Summer's theory. She imagined zones for each metal, in rings around the hemisphere, corresponding to the local temperatures. Here on the edge, where Iota shone at a very shallow angle through thousands of kilometers of Australia's thin atmosphere, they found zinc. Farther in, they would find pockets of plutonium, which melted at 640, or radium at 700.

Summer's real goal, something they would not be able to

see on this short trip, was what she imagined covering thousands of square kilometers at the center of this hemisphere, something that a satellite could confirm if only the company would outfit one to withstand the rigors of a trip so close to Iota: an ocean of molten metal. She imagined building a raft of platinum and pushing it onto the ocean, using incredibly light beryllium oars to paddle out over the slow, viscous waves. She'd never been on a body of water; no one around Iota had. But somewhere over the horizon was a place more exotic and wonderful than any ocean on Earth. It was what she imagined Heaven might be like.

None of this was valuable or practical from the viewpoint of the company. But Summer had determined there was a way to get the company to allow her to visit this place. Dotting Australia were small amounts of uranium, melting point 1135°C. And since uranium was, strangely, not very dense, it would float to the surface of the ocean. The oars of Summer's fantasy boat would cut through the thin layer of dark gray, revealing the brilliant depths beneath. Off the back of the boat would hang a net, a very fine net, which would catch only uranium, pulling the precious metal out of the ocean dozens of kilograms at a time. One lazy afternoon ride could do the work of ten months of drilling and extracting and refining.

Summer wanted to run toward the slanting rays of Iota, past aluminum falls and magnesium springs, splashing through creeks of antimony laced with tin. She wanted to follow a riverside where silver flowed brighter than the sky, the river widening to a delta and emptying into the ocean, shining silver intertwining with dull uranium in a strange dance. Farther out, away from the shores, the dusky surface would be unsullied by silver or copper or tin. For kilometers on end, as far at the eye could see, the subtle waves of the uranium blanket would hide fathomless expanses of pure, liquid gold.

"I can't believe it's real," said Summer, staring down at the little pool.

"It is real," said Gregor, "and you knew it."

Summer and Gregor turned to one another, seeing only featureless helmets. They paused, enjoying the moment, though the cameras lied, telling them that they were face to face. Then, as one, they looked away, from each other and from the blinding light streaking over the horizon. Walking back, dawn became sunset.

On the way to the shuttle, the couple's conversation was much freer. Summer talked about her plans, sketching out entire communities living on the day side of Australia. Crawling around underground to mine for ores would soon be a thing of the past. Gregor agreed and expanded on the ideas with his knowledge of extraction. Before they knew it, they were surrounded by darkness. They had to use the radio to find the shuttle again.

When they got back to Darwin, they kept talking all the way back to the dorm. Without any conscious decision, Summer went with Gregor back to his apartment. It was Summer's first time with a man, and she was excited and frightened. It was wonderful. Afterwards, with Gregor snoring warmly next to her, as she fell asleep, she wondered at how simple it was. They liked each other, and they made love, and it felt right.

She didn't dream.

Now that her theory had been proven correct, the company was eager to realize a profit. It was easy for Summer to have Gregor assigned as a specialist on her project. Summer had secretly worried that Gregor wouldn't fit in with the R&D group, but his easy manner and quick wit won him many friends, friends that Summer had taken years to impress. She felt a quick stab of jealousy, but soon dismissed it. She felt that Gregor's successes were hers as well.

Weeks went by as the team put together the specifications for a four-person, week-long expedition into the day side. Summer's estimates on rate of travel with special-built vehicles said they could possibly go far enough to see molten silver flowing free through the mountainside. As she became more excited, Gregor became distracted.

The news from Asia wasn't good. European terrorists

were hitting military installations all over Gandhi. There
was a report of a failed attempt to detonate a nuclear device
on Ganges, and another report of an intercepted shipment
of biological toxins to Fuji. Europe's leader Labrack
denounced the methods of these terrorists, at least in
public, but he did not denounce their goals or their
patriotic fervor. His speeches became more and more like
rallying cries. And the Europeans were responding.

Some of the Australians were responding, too, Gregor
among them. The miners felt a kinship with the oppressed
farmers of Europe. They held meetings and gave speeches
of their own, aping Labrack's turns of phrase. They
programmed flyers and posted them all over Darwin.
Company security took down the loud, flashing
advertisements and issued a memo saying that political
demonstrations were against company policy. The rabble-
rousers put up more flyers, which were taken down,
followed by a more strongly worded memo.

The determination of the revolutionaries and the inertia
of the company bureaucracy kept this cycle going for six
weeks before the company realized the problem would not
go away. They targeted all the group members and
scheduled transfers for every one of them to distant domes
around the planet, or to the automated mines around Asia.

Summer told Gregor she would call in some favors and
have his transfer cancelled. He told her that she shouldn't
bother, because he was quitting. When she heard that,
Summer knew that Gregor was immersed too deeply in the
rebellious fervor of his cause. Employment with the
company wasn't a choice; it was a culture, a culture that
spanned the planet. Australia was the company and the
company was Australia. She told this to Gregor, trying to
snap him out of his daze, but it didn't work. He said he was
leaving to join the workers of Europe in their struggle.

This was a blow to Summer. She didn't know what to
think or what to feel. Shock turned to grief, then sadness.
Anger turned to rage, then blew itself out. It wasn't simple,
like she thought. It wasn't enough to love someone, and
have him love you back. There had to be more than love to

forge a connection that could handle the stresses of life. Without something strong to keep you together, whatever bound you and your lover would break apart like graphite, splintered and cracked and crumbling away.

She told him she would miss him and then walked away.

He sent her an e-mail with his departure information, and asked her to see him off.

She didn't respond.

In the lab, day after day, Summer built the foundation and frame of her dream. She oversaw the design of ceramic and metal buggies that could roll over the bright, rough landscape on the other side of the planet. She watched two coworkers build a mockup of an inflatable habitat. She single-handedly drew up the plans for a one-person dingy to float on any lake or sea that they found. And she looked at Gregor's empty chair a thousand times a day.

Summer didn't know what to do, and she didn't have anyone to ask. Should she bear the pain and try to forget about Gregor, or should she swallow her pride and her fear and try to talk him out of his plan to leave the planet? Every hour, almost every minute, she evaluated the choices, and their repercussions, and their costs and benefits and risks. There was no end to the number of scenarios that she ran through, ranging from the banal to the baroque, from the painful to the joyous. And over and over, she looked back at that empty chair.

In the last week before Gregor was to leave, her focus was divided between the chair and the calendar, each boxed day glowing with possibility of reunion and tinged with the promise of pain. She waited for Gregor to call, to write, to visit, but she knew it wasn't in him to follow a dead trail. That was one of the things that made him good at extraction. And perhaps at revolution, as well.

On the last day, Summer's attention left the chair and calendar. Her eyes were glued to the clock. She told herself that with just a little more time, she would figure it out. She would learn what she had to do to make everything right and make them both happy again. She willed the seconds to stop ticking. She prayed for God to stop time for her. But time didn't stop. The hour approached faster and faster. Gregor's liner was scheduled to leave at 13:45.

Before her relationship with Gregor, Summer had analyzed other couples as best she could to try to learn the ins and outs, the rules, the traditions of romantic interaction. The only rule that seemed to apply more than fifty percent of the time was that relationships that lasted many years bred cynicism. Married men and women joked often about the crushing demands of their spouses, postulating aloud how wondrous breaking off the union would be. They were jokes, Summer realized, but for them to be so common, so well thought out, so persistent, she assumed there was a grain of truth to them. Something about people turned the blissful early days of a liaison into a drudgerous chore to be tended to. She saw it time and again.

Then she thought about Ilena and Jinpeng, her adopted parents. They never made jokes about being bored or disgusted by each other. They were always happy together, even during the worst of times. She had seen them make each other laugh a thousand times, and seen them steal surreptitious kisses when they thought their new daughter wasn't looking. They managed to keep their love alive for years.

And then she thought about her parents who, until this moment, she had never considered to be a couple in love. But they were. With only scant memories of the little time they could spare their precious Summer, she remembered two people whose love for their daughter was only matched by their love for each other. Their simultaneous death, such a blow to a little girl of eight, was, Summer now realized, a blessing for her parents. Neither had to ever live without the other.

At 13:30, Summer ran out of the lab. She ran down the street and across the dome. She kept running into the port.

The ceiling of the building was transparent, so as she ran in, she could see Gregor's shuttle leaving, taking him and the other passengers up to the orbiting interplanetary liner. She scanned the faces in the crowd, hoping desperately that he had changed his mind, that he had missed his connection, that he had tripped and broken something and couldn't make it onto the shuttle, anything that would *keep him here*.

Gregor wasn't there.

She stood in the middle of the lobby, paralyzed, numb. She didn't feel anything at all now. She was just empty. She gazed absently through the roof at the brilliant stars, one of which was moving quickly, taking her last chance for happiness away from her.

Then, something odd happened. The pinpoint shuttle winked out. Summer blinked, thinking it was a trick of her eyes. But it wasn't. The glow of the shuttle's engines was gone. A stab of fear that something had destroyed it hit her in the stomach, but she realized that destruction like that would have made a flash. The ship had simply gone dark.

There it was again. It was back. But it wasn't going the same direction. It was going the opposite direction. It grew larger. It was coming back.

Summer's heart started beating faster. Her breathing sped up. Cold sweat sprouted all over her body. It was a miracle. God had sent her a solid uranium miracle: a second chance.

A change in the air around her distracted Summer from her revelation. People weren't bustling through the port anymore. They were congregated near the building's support poles, looking up at the viewscreens. Summer moved to one and watched the news report with everyone else.

Europe had destroyed the beam assembly orbiting Iota. The beam was the only real-time communication conduit from this system to Earth, and they had destroyed it. If the concept of quitting the company had shaken Summer, the destruction of the beam sent her spinning. It was like the ground under you, something you expected to be there every day, even if it wasn't of particular importance to you. She had followed the news from Earth far less closely than the news from Asia or Europe, but the idea that it just *wasn't there* anymore was stunning.

"It's war," said Gregor. He was standing beside her now, his shuttle having landed and emptied. All traffic off the planet was temporarily suspended.

"War?" asked Summer.

"I can't go anywhere right now."

She grabbed him by the arms and turned him to her, face to face.

"I don't want you to go anywhere at all," she said, the tumultuous day making her bold. "I love you and I want you to stay with me and spend the rest of your life with me."

Gregor didn't answer. He looked in her eyes, searching. She looked back, hoping he'd find whatever he needed to find to believe her, to agree with her, to stay with her. A slow smile touched his lips, and he pulled her into a fierce embrace.

Maybe it was that simple, after all. Maybe love was enough, if it was strong enough and if you could say it out loud. Summer didn't feel sad or angry or frightened. She felt happy and she felt warm.

# REBELLION

Europe

April 15, 80
*(February 22, 2363)*

   Eliot McCanliss ran full tilt from the tram stop down to the farm, earning dubious looks from the homesteaders in their fields this morning. By the time he pounded his way up the path to the house, he was puffing and blowing into his oxygen mask. His mom was startled to see him in such a state as she peeled potatoes at the kitchen table.
   "What is it?" she asked.
   Eliot took a deep breath before answering in a wheezing voice:
   "War."

☼

   Eliot had only been eleven years old when Europe seceded from the Iotan Federation. It was faraway people talking about faraway things that didn't have much of an impact on a boy struggling with calculus and botany classes and with his intense crush on the spectacularly beautiful Mariah, a girl he knew at school.
   When Mariah started talking politics, Eliot followed

along for the sake of his hormones. After a while, though, the ideas started to really sink in. Why did Asia think they deserved special treatment? Weren't there a whole lot more Europeans than Asians? And didn't Europe produce pretty much all the food that the Iotans ate every day?

As Eliot and his classmates approached graduation, political dissent mutated from a cliquish fad for bored farm boys and girls into a real movement. They had meetings, both in person and over the radio; they handed out flyers; they gave speeches, aping the phrases used by Councillor Labrack. And the youth in Berlin weren't the only ones organizing. Large groups of university students in Copenhagen and Kiev screamed louder and longer than the Berliners about the inequities of economic structure in the system.

Eliot and his friends saw Anton Labrack as their hero, their mentor, maybe even their savior. They knew he couldn't really say what he wanted to say because he was in such a visible position, but they understood anyway. They knew what he wanted was a revolution, and that was what he was going to get.

✿

"War? What are you talking about?"

"Mom, it's finally started! We took out the beam assembly."

"You what?"

"Not me, Mom. C'mon. But our movement. Europeans. We blew up the Asians' link to Earth. I hear we're already making plans to intercept the resupply ship before it gets too close for the Asians to get their hands on it."

Eliot's mother wiped her hands on her apron and stood so she could stop her son from his frantic pacing around the room.

"This isn't going to help anyone, Eliot. It's just going to get people mad."

"Making people mad is the only way anything ever gets

done! You should know that!"

"I don't know any such thing. I know I sent you into town for a power cell for the tractor. Did you get that?"

"Mom, we just went to war! I can't be thinking about tractors at a time like this!" His mother had no concept of the scope of this. Iota would never be the same again.

"Well, young man, if we're at war, then the troops are going to have to eat, aren't they? And who's gonna feed them?"

Maybe she had a point, but it was such a come-down after the excitement of hearing the news. He did have work to do here and now. This was his farm, after all. He didn't have any brothers or sisters to help him do the work, and his mom... Well, she was still strong now, but someday she'd get too old to work.

"I'll get the power cell later. Right now, a bunch of the guys are having a party to watch the news over at Chad's place." Eliot felt ridiculous, a man of fifteen years asking his mother for permission to go out. Nonetheless, when she sighed and nodded her head, he ran out of the room like a child.

✿

Chad's family lived close to the Berlin dome. The Carlyle farm was newer than Eliot's home, enclosed under a makeshift mini-dome that they had to dismantle before each storm season and replace with those familiar radiation tarps; only a full-size city dome could withstand a major storm. Mr. Carlyle was sympathetic to their cause, so he let Chad's friends congregate, but he didn't stay to listen to their discussions. He was too busy in the fields.

By the time Eliot got there, two-dozen guys and girls around Eliot's age were already filling the house with talk of power struggle and demonstrations and even work stoppages. The radio was on, but the news hadn't changed since the initial announcement. They were eagerly awaiting Callahan's statement, which was expected in a couple of hours. They liked nothing better than shouting down that sanctimonious old bat.

"They'll cave," Mariah said to Eliot as he walked in. "They have to. They have to, don't they?"

"I don't know," he admitted. Mariah was still intoxicating to him, but she was seeing Chad now, and anyway, how could he get distracted by a wife—or worse, children—at a time like this? Running the farm was bad enough.

"We grow their food!" Mariah argued, subconsciously flipping her hair for him. Others walked past on the way to the kitchen for drinks and said "hi" to Eliot. He nodded to them.

"We seceded four years ago," Eliot reminded her, "and we still feed them. We can't not feed them."

"All we'd have to do is delay one shipment. One. They'd crumble." The hate in Mariah's eyes made her just the tiniest bit less attractive in that moment.

"Can we do that?" Eliot didn't like the idea of threatening to shut off Asia's supply of food. Not to mention Australia and Africa.

"I'm not saying we cut them off for good. I'm saying they live off their fat for a day or two."

"I guess." They'd have stocks saved somewhere. They had to have hedged against that possibility right after Labrack announced the secession years ago. They were smart enough to do that. No, stopping one shipment of food wouldn't starve anyone. It'd just make them think a little harder about what Europe's needs were.

And the Europeans weren't asking for the galaxy. They were asking for fair treatment. Fair payment for the valuable service they provided. Fair trade practices for American electronics and Antarctican water. Fair immigration policies for Africa. How could they not let more people live on Africa? It's not like the place was running out of indigenous life or anything.

The more he thought about their grievances, the angrier he became. He spared only a half-second to wonder what his eyes looked like just then.

"Eliot, walk with me!" Chad grabbed Eliot by the elbow and peeled him away from Mariah.

"We were just..." Eliot started to explain why he was spending so much time talking to Chad's girlfriend. Chad couldn't have cared less. He pulled Eliot to a quieter corner of the house where they could talk semi-privately. He leaned in, his ten centimeters of height advantage more noticeable than ever to Eliot.

"I'm taking this to the next level."

"Taking what to the next what?"

"This." He gestured to the impromptu party going on all around them. "The movement. My brother, Bill, you remember him?"

"He went to America a few years ago."

"Right. He says that's where things are really happening. Where people are planning to make statements that the system will hear, loud and clear."

"I don't get it."

"Look, I don't have specifics. I just know Bill, and he's a straight shooter, you know that."

Eliot didn't really know anything like that. He'd met Bill a couple of times when he was a kid playing with Chad after school. Bill was tall, like Chad, but a quiet guy, usually. Everyone was surprised when he left Europe to go to America, leaving the responsibility of the Carlyle farm to Chad. Now Chad sounded like he was talking about going out there, too.

"I want you to come with me," Chad said.

"What?"

"To America."

"I don't get it."

"I'm serious. Dead."

Eliot was stunned, to the point that he felt physically numb. He couldn't process it. The idea of leaving the planet? The idea of leaving his mother? The idea of leaving the farm? The idea that Chad wanted him to go along? And what about Mariah? Was she going? Would that make things worse... or better?

"That's a lot to think about," Eliot said. The room

seemed too loud, the air too thick to breathe properly. He hadn't even noticed Chad's hand on his shoulder, pinning him to the spot.

"I'm leaving next week. Think fast."

"And Mariah? She's okay with this?"

Chad leaned in even closer, to the point where Eliot could smell what he'd had for breakfast. "She doesn't know, so keep it under your hat, okay?"

Eliot looked around for prying ears, but the room was far too loud for their quiet conversation to carry to anyone. "She's not going?"

Chad answered with a dismissive shake of the head.

That added a whole new level of complexity to this decision. If Mariah was staying behind, and Chad was leaving... Did he have a chance with her? Was she the one he might settle down with, have some kids, carry on the family tradition that his great-great-grandfather had started back when the colony was first founded?

Someone near the radio called for everyone to quiet down. Callahan was about to speak. They all crowded around the table to listen. Eliot was glad for the distraction.

✧

Eliot walked home in a bit of a daze. The questions zipped around in his head, bouncing around without actually getting him anywhere. He needed to calm down and figure this thing out. What he'd been offered today... it was a chance of a lifetime! The opportunity to leave for an exotic land and change your entire life didn't come along every day. But that didn't mean it was necessarily a good thing...

He walked in the door with his mind whirling; his thoughts were as far as possible from the question of:

"Did you get the power cell?"

His mother was sitting near the stove, mending socks.

"I told you I'd get it later, Mom."

"Is it not later? I think it is later."

"I meant tomorrow."

"The fields aren't going to plough themselves, Eliot." She wasn't trying to be difficult. He knew that. She was trying to be helpful, trying to show him where his priorities should be... but now was not the time.

"We weren't going to plough the fields until next week anyway, so what's the point in nagging me about the power cell now?"

The annoyance in his voice was a notch higher than usual. Mom looked at him with a careful eye.

"Eliot. What's wrong?"

He was almost out the living room door, almost to his room, but he stopped. He was never quite sure why he stopped, but that decision ended up changing his life:

"Mom, what d'you think of Mariah?"

Mom put on that look that Eliot knew only too well. She wanted to say something mean, but she knew she had to temper it. It was the look she gave Mrs. Donovan at church when the nice old lady asked what Mom thought of her new hat, which was certainly god-awful ugly, but Mom couldn't say that to the pastor's wife. That look told Eliot everything he needed to know about what Mom thought of Mariah.

"She's going to make Chad a nice wife someday," she said. The unsaid addendum—"and not you"—came through clearly.

"They're gonna break up," Eliot said.

"Really... Well, I suppose Chad could do better." Eliot smirked, thinking of how catty his mother could be, when she was so convinced Grandma Juliette was the shrew in the family.

"You don't like her."

"Eliot, don't put words in my mouth."

"I'm telling you what I think. I think you don't like her."

"She's got a head full of ideas and not enough sense to keep them to herself."

"Mom!" That wasn't like her. Eliot realized Mom really didn't like Mariah. Of course, just today, Mariah had floated the idea of withholding food from Asia to make a political point. But that was justified... Wasn't it?

"I don't like the direction this conversation is going, Eliot."

"You're the one taking it in a nasty direction. I happen to agree with a lot of her ideas."

"You do not." She said it so simply, so certainly. As if she knew Eliot better than he knew himself. "You think you do because she's a pretty girl, but you know it's all nonsense." She didn't even look up from her knitting. She was being so... dismissive. Eliot was sick and tired of being treated like a child. Unfortunately, his instinctual response was to lash out like a child.

"Dad liked her."

The knitting stopped. They didn't talk very much about Eliot's father, Drake McCanliss. He'd died a little over three years ago in a tractor accident. Eliot sometimes wondered if Mom even missed him.

"Don't do that," Mom said.

"Do what?"

"Use him that way."

"You do it enough."

"I do not!"

"'Eliot, mend the tarps. Eliot, fix the tractor. Eliot, there's a leak in the roof.'" His sing-song inflection wasn't complementary.

"You're not making any—"

"Those are the things that Dad always did. You never ask me to sew or cook or can. You want me to do what Dad did. You're always reminding me that I need to be more like him."

"You should be more like him! He wouldn't act like a child over something as trivial as a girl!"

"He never did anything like that because of you?"

"That's different."

"Because Mariah's different, you mean."

"Yes."

For some reason, the argument paused. Eliot had to admit Mom was right. Mariah was different. She wouldn't have the dedication to sit and mend socks or balance ledgers or do a hundred other things that Mom did to keep this farm running smoothly. Eliot dropped into a chair at the kitchen table, thoughts churning again. If a life on the farm with Mariah wasn't the answer? Then...

"Son, I'm sorry." Mom sat next to Eliot. He barely noticed when she took his hand. "I know it's been tough on you since Dad died."

Maybe going to America with Chad was a good idea after all. He never loved the farm the way Mom did.

"But you've stepped up and handled your responsibilities like a man."

It would feel right doing something about Europe's problems, rather than just talking about them.

"I never told you this, but your grandmother blamed the farm for your father's death. I'm glad you understand that she—"

"The farm didn't kill Dad. Asia did," he said, with words like acid.

"I'm sorry?" She didn't understand.

"Mom, I've got to go." Eliot left the kitchen to go pack his things.

"Eliot, you just got back. Where are you going now?"

In his room, he stuffed clothes haphazardly into a duffel bag he'd inherited from his father. The bag was sturdy enough, though it seemed old. He could just barely make out the word "Icarus" on the side in faded letters. Mom appeared in the doorway.

"You're packing? Why are you packing?"

"Uncle Gerald's sons should be able to help out on the farm. He's certainly got enough of them." Eliot picked through a handful of books on his dresser and grabbed a couple of his favorites. He tossed them in the bag.

"I don't understand what you're doing, Eliot. Are you eloping with Mariah? Is that it? You don't have to do that."

"No. She's staying behind." He'd have to get another radio. Mom would need his. He dropped his portable computer in the duffel. He hefted the bag. It wasn't too heavy.

"Behind? Where do you think you're going?

Copenhagen? Did Grandma put ideas in your head?"

"I'm going to America."

Mom couldn't think of anything to say to that.

"It'll be okay," he said, and kissed her on the cheek. He put on his coat and his oxygen mask and left the farm.

✿

Chad was pleasantly surprised to see Eliot on his doorstep.

"I hope I'm making the right decision," Eliot admitted. Chad clapped him on the shoulder.

"We both are. Just got a message from Bill. He's moving his operation to Washington. He's got friends up there."

Eliot nodded. Soon, he'd be making Europe—all of the Iota System—a better place.

# SOLSTICE

Iota Horologii

June 19 – July 25, 125
*(November 9 – December 25, 2423)*

Waking up in the freezer wasn't what I expected. I was lying in that slush, breathing through a tube, for an hour before the lid tilted up and I squinted into the bright fluorescents of Bay 73. If our bay was being thawed out, I knew that we must have been in the Iota System for several months. We were probably orbiting Gandhi right now, a shuttle en route to *Telperion* to pick up my squad for posting in the capital.

I sat up, half-frozen blue sludge dripping from my head and arms. I didn't wait for the technician to pull the tube. I yanked it out of my throat in one swift, painful motion. The woman who had woken me was blonde, young, and pretty. I didn't yell at her the way I wanted to. This was a piss-poor operation to make me wait like that, but I'd save my comments for the Immigration Manager who was supposed to oversee all aspects of colonial arrival.

"Here, let me help you," the woman offered. I shook my head and hopped over the side onto the metal deck, thankfully padded with a rubber mat to insulate my feet. I wiped off as much of the freezing gel as I could and noticed that none of the 999 other chambers in Bay 73 were opened, just mine.

"What the hell's going on?" I asked.

"You'd better come to the bridge," she said. She looked young, but she didn't sound it.

My name is Captain Jonah Lexicott, ECAF. I spent most of my career in urban skirmishes around the Solar System. Since I never got killed, and I did a good job on every mission I was assigned, I was promoted up through the ranks to Captain. This is as far as I want to go. I want to know every soldier under my command, so I can shoot the shit with them during the down times, know what to expect from them in the rough times, and not sound like a damn fool when I write one of those letters no commander wants to write.

Leading a squad of Rangers on the *Telperion* resupply mission to Iota was a plum assignment that I wasn't too proud to petition for. I've always wanted to go to an out-system colony, and Iota, by all accounts, was one of the best. Four terraformable worlds, rich mineral resources, and a lean, mean Government Council that kept the popular view in mind but didn't get bogged down in a legislative mess like Earth was with its thousand squabbling Senators.

When *Telperion* left Earth, the common wisdom held that the military situation around Iota was stable, nearly perfect. A handful of terrorist incidents peppered the news a few decades earlier, carried out by some sort of radical environmentalist movement, but it had been quiet for years. Of course, the sudden infusion of another hundred thousand Earthers into an insular population that couldn't number more than a half-million by now, that kind of thing generates tension on both sides. Beefing up the Iotan Army, even if only with my squad of twenty, wasn't a bad idea.

I just hoped that the local Generals didn't have their heads *too* far up their asses.

The bridge of the ship was a huge disappointment. A round room, all gray metal and black plastic, with one control station in the center. No self-respecting science fiction movie would look like this. I cinched up the robe the woman had given me, even though the room was pleasantly warm. The man sitting in the big chair turned when I came in. He stood, tall, thin, as blonde as the woman. He offered his hand and a tight smile.

"Captain Lexicott, I'm Robert. You've already met Francesca."

"Good to meet you," I said, not meaning it. "What's up?"

Robert moved from the chair and offered it to me. I almost refused, but they were being very serious, so I decided to play along. I realized now they were the ship's android pilots, and androids are usually built with a solid sense of humor, which was necessary on the long jaunts they took. There was no humor in the room now. Their tone brought up my guard; I expected bad news.

Robert pushed a button on the console, and a hologram of the Iota System appeared. I knew it well from briefings that, at least to me, were only days ago. It should have taken *Telperion* about sixty-five years to get here. But then, I was assuming that *here* was Iota. I had an urge to walk over to the window in the floor, but I figured the androids knew how to tell me what they wanted to tell me.

"This is the Iota System as it was when we left Earth."

"As it was?"

Francesca joined the conversation. "Five years after our launch, the beam from Earth to Iota was broken." That shook me. I hadn't heard of a beam breaking before.

"How?"

"At the time," Robert said, "the best guesses were unanticipated supernova blast from Iota or malfunction of the beam assembly."

"I'm guessing neither of those happened." Robert and Francesca shared a look. Francesca nodded, and Robert pushed another control.

The hologram of the system changed dramatically. In fact, it took a careful look to recognize that it was the same one. I gaped, then turned to the couple.

"Tell me."

✧ ✧

*Telperion*, like all the colonization ships, was built for the convenience of a very small crew. One stateroom and one bridge on the lowest level, thirty levels of freezing bays, and another bridge and stateroom up top. Everything else—shuttles, colonists' storage, fuel cells—hung off the outside of the cylindrical ship like parasites. The living space wasn't designed to comfortably house twenty-two people. As my newly awakened squad wandered onto the bridge, they found places to lean or squat. Some just sat on the cool metal floor. Their mood was positive, but not as boisterous as it would have been under normal circumstances. They knew something was up.

Sergeant Carlson was keeping a close eye on the troops. Private Gallo was the loudest, cracking jokes that were old when we left, getting his best laughs from himself. Private Brady, the closest thing we had to a bookworm, took in the details of the bridge, then walked by herself to look out the window in the back. I had already looked. There was nothing to see.

Once the fifteen men and four women were all accounted for, Robert and Francesca came into the room and stood nearby. I would need their expertise for some of this briefing, but the bad news had to come from me. I nodded to Carlson, and she called for quiet. Everyone hushed up without comment, even Gallo.

"I'm sure you realize that something is going on, and I'm going to explain it to you now. Our original mission was to help maintain the stability of the Iota System. That mission has changed."

Using a remote, I started up the holographic Iota program.

"On February 22, 2363, Earth lost contact with Iota." The scene zoomed in on the north pole of the star. Floating above was the beam assembly, a satellite ten meters across, shaped like a melted tea cup, which orbited the star and held a live communications link with a sister satellite orbiting the Sun. "We believe, after reviewing the data received from Iota before contact was broken, that terrorists from the planet Europe destroyed the beam assembly—" The satellite exploded. "—as a reprisal for some unknown act of the Iotan military."

I had their undivided attention now. They sensed battle coming.

"What we know about the sequence of events that followed is the result of research done by our pilots during the last leg of the journey here." The view of the hologram swept over to Africa, the whole planet a uniform muddy-gray. "On September 3, Africa exploded." The computer provided a dramatization of the destruction of the planet, reproduced without sound, which was appropriate, but unsettling. Fire swept across the planet, gray turning to burnt orange, rising to yellow, then white. It trembled for a moment, then the planetary crust cracked apart like a fragile Christmas ornament. Pressurized red magma beneath the crust forced the sphere to shatter, sending pieces of burning crust hurtling away at terrible speed. The magma itself flew in all directions, but slower, soon settling into a bloody smear, staining the planet's orbital path with red hot debris that would take a thousand years to cool.

The room was totally silent. The destruction of an entire planet was beyond our experience. It took the squad a moment to realize what they had seen. Brady spoke up.

"How can a planet explode like that? We don't have a weapon anywhere near that destructive."

I looked to Robert, who was the expert on what little we knew about the Iota situation.

"Thank you, Captain. After reviewing several of the scientific journal articles sent from Africa to Earth, I believe I've found the cause of the explosion." He went on to explain that the biosphere of Africa was laced with high concentrations of native petroleum. A single conventional warhead would have been more than enough to cause the devastation we witnessed in the simulation.

Now the squad's blood was really up. The European terrorists, who had seemed like kind of a joke on Earth,

now loomed in their minds as a major threat to peace. I had
to make a choice: should I cut to the chase and tell them
what waited for them outside the ship, or keep going,
describing all of this like some sort of Homer, milking
tragedy for drama? Looking at Sergeant Carlson, who was
also hearing this for the first time, I saw that she was
emotional, but intent, focused on the facts, and not jumping
to any conclusions yet. I knew she could control the soldiers
if necessary.

"Thank you, Robert," I said, taking over again. For now,
I'd be Homer. "On December 15, something happened on
America." The view switched to the monstrous America, a
hundred years of terraforming efforts barely having begun
to change the planet's atmosphere. "Another terrorist
group—again, we assume it was Europeans—set a nuclear
charge here—" We zoomed toward a narrow valley that
sliced north/south through the planet. "—in this valley
known as the Pit of Hades." A flash of light came from the
crevice, then lava began to boil out of the crack. Slowly, the
lava forced the crack to widen, breaking open the planet
like an egg. The far ends of the valley ripped open the crust
to the north and south, almost to the poles. Like a mouth
opening, the valley continued to spread, the interior of the
planet spilling out over the surface. At the same time, on
the far side of the planet, the crust wrinkled and buckled,
collapsing into the emptying interior. America didn't quite
manage to turn itself inside out. After barely a minute, one
half of the planet was seething, boiling lava, and the other
half was a hemisphere-sized mountain range, tilted and
broken, the tallest peaks collapsing under their own weight.

I wanted to stop, but I had to finish the briefing, if only
to cool the rage that I saw on every face, even Brady's.

"What happened next, we don't really understand, but it
happened hours after America was attacked." I didn't say
any more. I let the pictures speak.

The computer showed us the system from a distance
again. Without warning, the planet Asia burst into flame.
Sheets of glowing hot gas blew off the planet at half the
speed of light, and the core lit up with an intense blue fire.

There were gasps from the squad as the simulated blast cascaded over them. All ten moons of Asia, including the large ones, Gandhi and Azuka, were reduced to radioactive dust.

There was always the assumption on Earth that Jupiter was close to being a star on its own. If it was only a little bigger, it might have made it. I even read a story once where someone managed to turn it into a star, which seemed strange and exciting when I read it. Now, watching the same thing happen to Asia, a planet a little more than twice as massive as Jupiter, it wasn't exciting anymore. It was terrifying. Even the fact that it was only a computer simulation didn't blunt the impact. Nearly a quarter of the population of Iota, one hundred twenty thousand people, died in a matter of moments when Asia was transformed from a planet into a star. Unfortunately, the show wasn't over.

Europe, locked in a tight orbital resonance with Asia, was just ahead of the gas giant in its own orbit when the shower of superheated gas pelted the smaller planet. Europe's largest moon, DeGaulle, was knocked against the edge of Europe like a billiard ball. The now deformed moon spun off, taking a small chunk of Europe with it. The side of Europe that faced Asia now glowed red, an entire hemisphere set ablaze. The force of the blast knocked the planet out of its orbit, shooting it off at a tangent. Europe's original orbit was nearly circular, 483 Earth days long. It was now in a highly eccentric and unstable orbit that wouldn't bring it close to Iota again for 250 years. Ironically, the new orbit would also, several thousand years later, send the planet crashing headlong back into Asia, as if in retaliation for what the new star had done to it.

Australia, the small planet nestled in close to Iota, was also near conjunction with Asia, but its fate was even worse. The blast that had accelerated Europe away from Iota shoved Australia *backward*, reversing its orbit. It was now circling Iota in the opposite direction, but not quite as fast. It was playing a losing game with the star, spiraling in toward her. Now, sixty years on, it lived in Iota's corona, and was close enough to be kissed by some of the larger prominences. The planet was now little more than a white-hot molten ball of minerals. It was doomed to be completely enveloped by Iota in just over a hundred years' time.

The boiling remains of Africa, still settling into their eventual orbits, were dispersed even farther. The Iota System never had an asteroid belt, but it would soon enough.

Even massive America and distant Antarctica were battered by the destruction of Asia, setting both planets' orbits wobbling.

The Iota System was so changed it seemed like the ending of a bad joke. How many terrorists does it take to destroy a solar system? Humanity's third extra-solar colonization effort was reduced to ashes and flame in less than a year. And this antiseptic astronomy lesson didn't come close to describing the terrible human cost of the war. Nearly half a million people were burned or buried or frozen.

I let the newly changed system continue to revolve around the room while the troops took in the news. Each was shocked, as if from battle fatigue. In ninety seconds or so I had reviewed enough devastation to fill a decent mythology. I let them try to catch up for a few moments, but I didn't want them wallowing in despair.

"Now we're on a rescue mission," I said.

A few heads bobbed up. Private Sharples, usually a quiet man, spoke up now.

"Rescue who?"

Heads turned to me, looking for some good news. "There are three sites to check." I clicked the remote again, and our view backed away from Iota, bringing us close to the renegade Europe, now cold and dark and distant.

"We're vectoring *Telperion* toward Europe now. The hemisphere that faced Asia during the explosion is certainly lifeless, but the other side may have intact settlements running on power reserves."

I clicked again, and we returned to the inner planets. I

walked over to America, which looked now like a strange piece of candy, half chocolate, half cherry. I pointed to her only moon.

"There were over five thousand people living on Washington when we left Earth. The destruction of America would not have impacted them directly. When Asia ignited, they were in America's shade. There could still be people there."

One last click took us out to the far side of the system.

"Antarctica. Sixteen thousand people lived out here. Our best chance to find anyone still alive in the Iota System is here."

Filled with a new sense of purpose, the squad was almost smiling. They weren't happy, but they had a mission. Even better, they had a mission that didn't involve taking lives, but saving them. I just hoped there were still some left for them to save.

◇ ◇

Europe had three major cities and hundreds of smaller settlements strewn around the globe. The atmosphere hadn't yet become breathable for animals, so every locale was domed and pressurized. The smaller settlements were built beneath a metal framework covered with reactive plastic sheeting that held in oxygen but allowed other gasses to breathe. It also served as a kind of lens, multiplying the heat from Iota several fold. The setup was designed to be dismantled before each biannual storm season, during which the inhabitants would ride it out for a few weeks in underground bunkers living off stores of energy, food and oxygen. With Europe now more than thirty AU from Iota, the sunlight on her surface was minimal at best, and the bulk of her atmosphere, both new and original, had been blown off by the force of Asia's explosion. The minor settlements were not a viable place for survivors.

Of the three main cities, running on nuclear power and domed with more permanent materials, the two largest were Kiev and Copenhagen. Both of these cities were on the eastern hemisphere and bore the full brunt of Asia's transformation. No one could have possibly survived. This reduced our rescue possibilities for Europe to one place: Berlin.

Private Grant flew the shuttle through the darkness toward Berlin. We passed over gently rolling plains that would have been perfect for farming, if the ground was seeded properly. A handful of automated stations dotted the landscape, designed to process the rough brown sand into fertile soil, all now lying dormant. The plain sloped down to the edge of a continental shelf. It was there on the brink that the city was built.

Two connected domes rising a hundred meters into the sky covered the city of Berlin. Berliners had high hopes that their city would be the jewel of the western hemisphere, nestled between valuable farmland and what would eventually have been the second largest ocean on the planet. The city looked like it was sleeping under the starry sky. No lights were burning, but that didn't mean anything. Lighting outdoors would be a waste of energy—energy that was better spent heating buildings and recycling oxygen and water. We had high hopes as we set down the shuttle.

The port was near the intersection of the two domes. I broke us into three teams: Grant and Hayes remained with the shuttle; Carlson took eight troops into the north dome; I took the rest into the south dome. We would sweep the area quickly and be back at the shuttle in two hours, hopefully with survivors in tow.

✪✪

"Hey, Brady?"

"Yes?"

"You believe in ghosts?"

"Knock it off, Gallo," I said. I didn't want people getting spooked. The last thing we needed was a firefight against shadows. I had considered leaving our weapons on

*Telperion*, but somehow that didn't sit right with me. Each soldier carried a Kalashnikov 3mm magnetic rifle over his or her shoulder and a SW 10mm pistol in a side holster. We were prepared, just in case.

"I'm just saying, is all. It's spooky, y'know?"

"Gallo, take Tate and DePalma and check out that building." I pointed at a blocky structure up ahead that looked like a college dormitory. Gallo was smart enough to take the hint and do as he was told without further comment. The south dome was laid out like a college campus, with the dormitory at the center and other large buildings in a ring around it. Dozens of single-story buildings sat closer to the edge of the dome. I sent Hayes, Silverberg and Dunbar around to the left. Brady, Sharples and I went right.

Berlin's two domes were still intact, but the atmosphere was long gone, escaped either through an open hatch or a million little cracks. The temperature inside the dome was close to a hundred below zero. The starlight was bright enough to get around, but we wore low-light goggles just to be sure.

After so many years away from Earth, on the Jovian moons and Titan, I was used to the disconnection from my surroundings. No sound of our steps on the rough concrete roadways. No crickets or birds or the sad creaking of doors that always seems to come with abandoned places. No feeling of wind on your back, nor the scent of burnt carbon. Only the sound of breathing from Brady and Sharples and the bleak monochrome cityscape. Gallo's talk of ghosts was inappropriate, but understandable. Training allowed us to focus on what we saw, but it was hard to ignore the missing inputs from our other senses.

I tried to make this a learning experience for Brady. She was the least experienced Ranger in the unit.

"Tell me what you see, Brady."

Sharples gave me a look as if to say, "She won't see much, sir."

"Well, we haven't seen any bodies in the street, so they didn't lose pressure quickly. None of these smaller buildings have bodies, either, so it looks like they had time to get into one place before—"

She didn't want to say before they died. We all wanted to find survivors. But after sixty years?

"What's the most likely place to find anyone?"

Brady pointed her weapon over a nearby factory toward the building I had sent Gallo to check. The dormitory dominated the skyline from every angle. I gave Sharples a look. He shrugged.

We investigated three labs and four factories, all of which were shut down in an orderly fashion. No sign of hurried exit. A place for everything and everything in its place. It was conceivable that the Berliners had evacuated the city for somewhere else, but where? This was the only permanent dome remaining on the planet, and taking a shuttle back to Iota would have been suicide with the radiation that Asia had thrown all over the inner system for the first few years after its rebirth.

We completed our semicircle and met up with Hayes and his group after forty minutes, then the six of us headed north to the dormitory to help Gallo. Before we got there, Gallo sent us a message.

"Place is empty, sir."

We were regrouping outside the dormitory when we got a call from the other dome. It was Carlson. I could tell from her tone she didn't have good news.

"We found them, Captain."

○ ○

The northern dome was designed like the southern, with a main residence building, fifteen stories tall, ringed by factories, then smaller labs and workshops. Carlson and her eight troops were all milling around on the first floor of the dormitory. Like the rest of the city, everything here was clean and tidy. There was no sign that a disaster had occurred other than the dark emptiness.

None of the troops waiting for us looked good. The

sergeant led me to a stairwell and we walked down. It was pitch black down there. The goggles did us no good. Carlson powered up a lamp, keeping it dim. That was enough to see everything.

The basement extended past the foundations of the dormitory, under most of the town. We stood at the foot of the stairs, near the center of the room. It was almost a kilometer from one end to the other. Stacks of food, water, clothes and other supplies dotted the room, but mostly the room was filled with beds. Some were big, comfortable mattress beds. Some were funky futon contraptions. Most of them were bare-bones cots, steel bars and canvas.

Lying on almost every bed was a corpse. Thousands of them, rows and rows of calm, peaceful bodies. Young, old, healthy, weak. Certainly not all of the fifteen thousand people who were supposed to live here sixty years ago, but many thousands. This was where the remaining residents of Berlin had come to die. I was shocked by how serenely they had gone about it.

I gave Sharples and Brady the task of counting the dead. I told Holt and Burns to look for computer or written records so we could try to piece together when and how they died.

The rest of the team stayed up top and finished the sweep of the southern dome. But they found no one else.

Someone asked me later if we should have tried to bury the dead. I said that they already were buried, and left it at that.

✧✧

We knew there were no survivors, but I needed to find out anything I could about the war that destroyed the system, and particularly about the weapon that turned Asia into a minor star. It was more likely that the keys to those terrorist actions were lost when the planet's capital, Kiev, was destroyed, but I couldn't leave without trying to find some clues. Whoever they were, I knew they might still be somewhere in the system. They were a continuing threat to us, to Earth, to every human in the galaxy.

Our fuel consumption had to be carefully watched. Maneuvering in-system would take precious resources, and we still had a long journey back to Earth ahead of us. There was only time for one more trip to Berlin. We brought thirty-four personal journals and fifty-five intact computer drives back to *Telperion* before once again heading toward Iota.

☼ ☼

Francesca managed ship's operations, giving Robert time to research the materials from Berlin. We tried to keep out of their way as much as possible, creating a bivouac in one of the freezing bays. Along with the journals, we brought back as many stores of food, water and air from the Berliners' tomb as we could carry, enough to last us months if necessary.

Washington was still three days away when Robert called us back to the bridge for his analysis.

"Please remember that this briefing is based only on information from the files found in Berlin, so the viewpoint is quite pro-Europe," Robert warned. "But I believe it is instructive nonetheless." I nodded for him to continue.

"The situation around Iota was not as rosy as we were led to believe from their beam transmissions," he said. "Political turmoil began almost immediately as the bulk of the colonists were sent to Europe for terraforming and they realized that the third planet was not the Eden they were promised. The largest problem was the biannual conjunctions with the massive Asia."

"Not because it eclipsed Iota, I hope," I said. I would have zero patience with these Europeans if they started a war because they had trouble getting a tan.

"No. It was Asia's gravity. Even at that distance, the pull from the gas giant was significant: about six times the pull of the moon on Earth."

"That'd be some big tides," Gallo said.

"They had no oceans for tides. Once every two Europe years, their proximity to Asia caused planet-wide atmospheric storms that lasted five to six weeks. The Europeans tried to make the best of their situation, but after only a few decades, their discontentment was both widespread and passionate. Splinter groups calling for the large-scale colonization of Africa and emigration to Gandhi and Azuka eventually grew into a major force of European politics.

"Control of the beam assembly orbiting Iota was held solely by the Asian government, which censored every transmission to Earth for signs of unrest. The Asians feared how our resupply mission would have been structured if Earth knew what was going on here. Dissension in the Council on economic and political issues eventually led to the secession of Europe from the Iota Federation in 2367, the year we left Earth. America and Antarctica followed immediately thereafter."

That brought a murmur from the troops. More than one muttered the phrase *civil war*. I realized that many of our assumptions didn't make sense anymore.

"The destruction of the Iota beam five years later was not a reprisal by Europe for an Asian attack. It was a preemptive strike."

"Why? What did they have to gain?" I asked.

"Europe was building their own beam to Earth," Robert said. "They wanted control of outsystem communication."

"Is that even possible? Sending a beam without a target?" Carlson asked.

"There would be a target: the assembly orbiting our Sun, which was tasked with maintaining the communication beam to Iota Horologii. That's why the Europeans had to destroy Iota's original beam, to make way for their own beam."

"When did the Europeans start building their beam?" I asked.

"Soon after their secession," Robert said.

"So," I said, thinking aloud, "it's five years after I secede, my beam is only a fraction of the way to Earth, and I decided to strike now? Why destroy it at that time?"

"Something else must have happened," Brady said. "Something Robert hasn't found yet."

"That is possible," Robert admitted, "though my review of the personal journals indicates it was a patriotic surge gone wild. The population of Europe was growing tired of a revolution with no clear positive result and wanted to see a visible sign of their power against Asia."

"Alright... Keep going," I said.

"Two months after the Asians' beam was destroyed, the Iotan military attacked and destroyed the European beam assembly. That appears to be the incident that triggered the destruction of Africa."

"It's mad," Brady said. "How could they kill everyone on an entire *planet* just because they lost some *hardware?*"

"It was a disproportionate response," Robert said. Brady glared at him. I started to wonder, not for the first time, if Robert's programmers had missed a subroutine or two. He didn't seem passionate about the carnage we were discussing. I watched Francesca, too, and saw she was keeping a close eye on her copilot. I made a mental note. Something there was worth investigating, but the issue at hand was the briefing.

"The other piece of news I have," Robert continued, "is that the nuclear bomb planted on America was placed there by Asian operatives."

"Asia?" Gallo said. "Why?"

"The attack on America was a direct reprisal for the destruction of Africa. A planet for a planet, you might say."

"Good God," Brady said. "You're saying that first, Europeans detonated the explosive on Africa, which destroyed it because it was like a bomb, waiting to go off—"

"I wonder if they knew what would happen," Gallo said.

"It seems likely," Robert said.

"Alright," Brady continued. "Then the Asians, as punishment, set off the nuclear device on America, which essentially destroyed it."

"It's clear they knew exactly what they were doing

there," Robert offered.

"So who blew up Asia?" Brady asked. The question was on all our minds.

"It appears to have been one of the rebel planets: Europe, America or Antarctica," Robert said.

"Antarctica. What do we know about them?" Gallo asked.

"Actually, Antarctica was friendly with everyone, since they were the major source of water for the entire system, which was desperately needed for terraforming. They did lean ideologically toward Europe and her cause. As a side note I would add that there was a widely held belief, completely without evidence, that Antarctica was withholding vital resources from the entire system."

"They were generous with their water, it sounds like," Carlson said. "What were they holding out on?"

"It was the water that many found suspicious," Robert said. "On Earth, the oceans are laced with small but significant amounts of deuterium and tritium, which of course is used for fusion. These hydrogen isotopes are completely absent from Antarctica's water. It was believed that they were hoarding the fusion fuel for themselves, letting the rest of the system extract its power from fissioning uranium."

"Sounds believable to me," Gallo said.

"Or it's just a local legend," Brady said.

"Until we know more," I said, "we have to assume that anyone might have destroyed Asia."

"The destruction of Asia could have been some sort of catastrophic accident as well, though that seems unlikely."

"The Asian system was destroyed less than one day after the explosion on America," I said. "It was no accident. Robert, do you have any better idea *how* it was done?"

Robert shook his head.

✿ ✿

Washington was similar in size to Earth's moon,

orbiting America every two months. It was quite a bit lighter in color than either our moon or America. Sort of a tan. No terraforming was attempted there, since the low gravity would eventually allow the atmosphere to escape into space. Rather, the moon was a key industrial location for America, since the planet's high gravity made mining and construction difficult. Rumor had it that the wealthier Americans would shuttle up to Washington to spas, taking a break from the crush of the large planet.

Washington's major city was Chicago, near the center of the planetside hemisphere. As before, we took a shuttle down and parked near the single dome. The layout of the city was similar to one of Berlin's domes. Though Chicago was a much smaller city than Berlin, home to only about two thousand people, I brought the same contingent of troops with me, leaving only Furillo and Carlson on *Telperion*.

While the Berliners had faced death with dignity and grace, the Chicagoans had not. We saw the first of many bodies in the shuttle port.

○○

"Captain, I think I've found something."
"Where are you, Brady?"
"Building 3, second floor."
The dome over the city was cracked, broken from the *inside*, it appeared, a sad detail that we never explained. Death had struck Chicago quickly and savagely. Bodies were strewn all over the circular promenade that ringed the central living facility. People had been caught at work in their labs and factory shops. Some had died in the middle of tasks, not understanding as the air became thinner and they found it harder and harder to breathe. Others understood their fate and fought their way to the dormitory, trampling their fellow citizens even as they themselves died.

The dormitory itself was even more unsettling. It appeared that very quickly after the dome cracked, all elevators and stairwells in the building lost their integrity to the near vacuum outside, leaving each floor to fend for itself. The third floor was the scene of a large-scale gunfight. The fifth floor showed signs of a group of people pushed to agonizing limits by starvation.

The tenth floor was mostly children.

There were horrifying tableaux everywhere that we tried to ignore to do our job. I was secretly pleased to be distracted from the frozen images of pain and went to find Brady.

Building 3 was on the north side of town. It looked like all the other buildings, a blocky amalgam of research facility and factory. There were stacks of silvery sheet metal just inside the main entrance, a few of which had been pressed with a complex crosshatch pattern. I ran a gloved finger over the design, then went upstairs.

Brady was sitting at a computer console, which she had wired to a power pack brought down from *Telperion*. Dozens of windows cluttered the computer screen, none of which made any sense to me. The floor of the lab was littered with metal shards and shavings. Leaning against one wall were dozens of precisely cut pieces of the same pressed metal that I had seen downstairs, each of these a regular seven-sided figure. On a table was one more, this one molded into an odd shape, a cross between a serving dish and an orchid. I reached for the thing when Brady cautioned, "Careful with that."

"Why? What is it?"

"It's a gravity mirror."

"A what?"

"A gravity mirror. A regular mirror reflects light. A heat mirror, like the fabric of our suits, reflects heat. This—" Brady stood and carefully picked up the dish. It must have massed at least twenty kilos. "—reflects gravity. That is, if the computer is right."

"How?"

"I'm not sure yet. Shall we give it a try?"

She was carefully holding the mirror with the dish facing up. She turned it over, the concave side facing down toward the surface of Washington, and she let it go. It didn't fall.

"What's the power source?" I asked, waving my hands over and under the floating mirror like a child trying to understand a magic trick.

"There is no power source. It's the material, a bizarre alloy of ten different metals, and the pattern on the surface, and the shape of the dish that makes it work. Washington throws its gravitons out, pulling anything with mass back toward it. But this mirror bounces the gravitons off. That's why it doesn't fall to the ground."

"Amazing. Get all the information you can."

"Captain!" It was Carlson, calling from *Telperion*.

"Go ahead, Carlson."

"There's something happening to Washington. It's changing orbit."

"It's what? Are you sure?"

"Yes, sir. It's falling toward America."

With all the destruction that had been visited the Iota System, I didn't want to take any chances of being caught in some final catastrophe.

"How much time do we have?"

"At this rate, it won't collide with the planet for something like... a thousand years."

"You're kidding me," I said.

"It just started moments ago, and we don't know what happened. It could accelerate. I recommend that you come back to *Telperion* as soon as possible."

I paused, looking at the gravity mirror. "Hold on, Sergeant."

I brushed the edge of the mirror. Like a poorly placed table cloth, the mirror slowly tipped over, then crashed to the floor.

"What's happening now?" I asked Carlson.

"It... It stopped. Washington's orbit is stabilizing. What happened?"

"I think we'll have an explanation soon." I punched buttons on the sleeve of my suit to hook in all the frequencies of the teams scouring Chicago. "Surface troops, listen in." I turned my attention back to Brady, who had been listening to the conversation. "You have an explanation, don't you, Brady?"

"It's bizarre, but yes, I think I know what happened." She gave the audience a quick explanation of the gravity mirror's function. "The mirror did bounce the gravitons from Washington off, but some of them bounced *directly* back at Washington. The mirror actually *pulled* Washington up, which means toward America. The pull wasn't drastic, probably only a few hundredths of a percent of the total gravity of the moon, but it was enough for Sergeant Carlson to notice."

"How could this little thing have that much power?" I asked.

"It's not a question of the mirror, it's a question of what the mirror is... mirroring. When Washington sends gravitons out, they carry one piece of information: the mass of Washington. That's why everyone and everything feels the same gravity on the moon's surface. They're all being bombarded by these same gravitons. But if you *reflect* those gravitons, you're reflecting something that carries that same information."

"It's like there's another Washington right there in the mirror," Carlson said.

"Yes. If the mirror was more efficient, it would be *exactly* like that. The mirror would have pulled Washington *much* faster."

"This is what they used to blow up Asia, isn't it?" Gallo asked over the radio.

There was a tide of murmuring on the radio after that comment. "Let's keep the channel clear," Carlson scolded. The chatter stopped.

"Captain, may I say something?" It was Robert.

"Certainly."

"The gravity mirror can clearly exert a pull on something, but Asia wasn't pulled apart. It underwent extreme compression, which caused fusion in the core, and hence it became a star."

Silence. Like any good schoolteacher, I let the silence spin out, waiting for someone to fill it with an answer.

Unlike a teacher, of course, I didn't already know what that answer was.

"The mirrors could have done it," Brady said. I looked over to her. She was smiling. "Imagine a thousand mirrors, all hanging above Asia, evenly spread out like... like dimples on a golf ball."

"A what?" Gallo asked.

"I've got it, Brady," I said. "Go ahead."

"They'd all pull a little bit, making Asia expand like a balloon."

"But that's not what happened," Carlson said.

"No, it is. It's what happened *first*. The Americans must have placed those mirrors months, maybe years earlier. They'd be too small to see from any of the Asian moons. But after America was destroyed, someone here on Washington... maybe someone sitting right at this desk... They pressed a button, and all at once, all the mirrors turned away from Asia."

I understood what she was saying, finally. She went on, "It's similar to the design of early nuclear weapons. You send a controlled blast into the uranium from all directions to compress it. The compression causes fission, which causes the explosion. Here, the mirrors would be pulling the planet from all directions, artificially expanding it. When they all stopped at the same moment, the planet would contract. If it imploded fast enough, the core would momentarily undergo enough pressure to start a fusion reaction. Asia exploded just like a nuclear bomb."

"This would work with only a thousand mirrors?" I picked the mirror up off the floor, now with a new respect, and fear.

"One moment," Robert said. We waited as he did his calculations. "Since Asia was so massive, nearly a star in its own right, it would only have taken 2,150 mirrors of the type you have there in the lab, based on the information I have."

Brady turned back to her monitor, flipping through windows. "I show here that this lab made eight thousand of them."

The discovery was as astonishing as it was terrifying. Nothing in history—not gunpowder nor the atom bomb nor ebola spray—could compare to the destructive capability of this. And judging by the lab Brady and I were in, it wasn't difficult at all. For the price of a few thousand kilos of metal, it was possible to devastate an entire solar system. I didn't think long about my next decision.

"Brady, have you transmitted any of the information from that computer out of this room?"

"No, sir."

"Erase it all."

"Excuse me?" Robert asked over the radio. "What did you say, sir?"

"I'm erasing all traces of this technology."

"You... You can't," was all Robert could come up with.

"I can and I am."

Brady looked up at me, unwilling to voice the question in her eyes. I nodded to her. She turned back to the computer and started killing all the files.

"Captain Lexicott, you don't have the authority to do this," the android said.

"I don't care. This knowledge ends here."

I placed the mirror on a workbench and rifled through the tools in the lab.

"Others will discover this," he continued. "It's better to have the knowledge now."

"No. It's not. It's better to delay it as long as possible."

There it was: a laser torch. The battery was dead, but I had a spare in my pack.

"Captain," Gallo said, "are you sure about this?"

The torch came to life with the new battery. I tuned it to its highest setting.

"Yes, Gallo. I'm sure."

"I'm just saying, if someone else is gonna have it, then—"

"Are you questioning my orders?"

"No, sir. But I'm just saying—"

"Private!" I said louder than necessary.

I run a very informal squad, something I learned from a captain I served with years ago. Interaction, discussion, even dissention can be a valuable tool for building a dynamic, cohesive unit. It is rare for me to snap at my troops. I prefer to guide, cajole, lean on them. The real discipline I leave to my sergeant.

But now, my tone made it clear that the discussion was over, and everyone knew it. I told myself I was putting Gallo back into line after letting him run a little too wild since he was thawed out. I told myself that this was too big a decision for a committee. But the truth was I was scared that someone might talk me out of destroying the mirror and the files, and I didn't want my squad to even try.

Robert was a different matter.

"Captain, you cannot unilaterally throw away such an important scientific discovery. Can you imagine the implications for construction and transportation alone? Think of a planet with no roads, colonized with cities that float above the ground, people traveling from place to place in weightless vehicles. The possibilities are astonishing!"

I began cutting the mirror into tiny shards, hopefully masking anything about its original shape. It was overkill, since I had already decided to destroy the entire lab as a precaution.

"Brady, make sure you reformat all those drives. I don't want someone retrieving that data."

"Yes, sir." She didn't sound happy about it, but Brady still didn't question me. Part of me wanted her to, but I was mostly glad she didn't. Robert refused to give up.

"Just because the knowledge can be used for destruction doesn't mean—"

"Not 'can be,' Robert. It *was* used for destruction," I interrupted. We would have to use a very high temperature explosive on the lab, I thought. It was just as important to erase any record of the intricate pattern on the surface of the mirror.

"You're right, of course. It was used to destroy, and hundreds of thousands of people were killed, and that's a terrible tragedy. But you can't walk away from this knowledge. Where would humanity be if we gave up on nuclear research just because you can make a bomb out of it? We would have no fusion. Earth would have run out of energy decades ago."

"Sergeant, disconnect Robert from this communications channel."

"Yes, sir."

"I protest this—" There was a snapping sound as Robert was cut off. Brady was finished with the computer and checked the next room, looking for any other records of the terrifying breakthrough.

"Captain?" she said. I wasn't very far into taking apart this thing, but I stopped to see what she wanted.

It was a storeroom. Brady was standing in the middle of a hundred sixty-two gravity mirrors.

✿ ✿

The squad seemed excited at the prospect of seeing something like this, and I couldn't blame them. We're all fascinated by destruction: the implosion of an old building, the power of a giant hurricane, even the horrible devastation of a nuclear weapon. Humans seem to be drawn to spectacles of chaos. At least for this show, no one was going to be hurt. Robert stewed at the back of the bridge as we all watched on the screen. Francesca had an arm around his shoulders, whispering something into his ear, but he seemed untouched by her.

Brady actually came up with the idea. The rest of the troops had all gotten onto the shuttle to stand by as she and I took the gravity mirrors out of the store room and spread them all out, face up, on the floor of the lab. We shared a look. I nodded. Then, as fast as we could, we turned each of the mirrors over. There wasn't enough room in the lab for them all to lie on the floor, so we stacked them, mirror after mirror hovering in mid-air, like some bizarre plate-spinning act. They were stacked six high in places.

They were heavy, and we both worked up a good sweat flipping every last one of the mirrors over until the room was a three-dimensional maze of the oddly twisted shapes.

It was almost funny as we tried to maneuver our way out of the room. We ran for the shuttle and it took off with time to spare.

That many mirrors all at once were enough to pull Washington so far out of its orbit that it impacted America only fifty-two minutes later, a few minutes after we had docked with *Telperion*. Robert and Francesca dutifully recorded the event for posterity, since no one had ever witnessed two such massive bodies colliding.

As chance would have it, Washington impacted America almost exactly between the molten lava side and the cracked landscape side. At the moment the moon touched the planet, two things happened. The cold mountainous side of America caught flame as the huge kinetic energy of the moon was transferred into heat. The fire swept nearly the whole way around the planet. On the other side, where America's surface was already soft and hot, a massive wave of lava flowed visibly across the red hemisphere, washing up on the far shore.

Washington itself slid sideways after the initial collision, towards the lava where the resistance was less, but it soon shattered into broken tan pieces, which continued to splatter over the entire disrupted face of America. Eventually, the moon was no longer distinguishable from the rest of the planet except as a colorful stain. The planet itself was ringing like a bell, and would continue to do so for millennia.

I was confident that the lab was destroyed.

✩✩

The trip out to Antarctica took us three weeks. That was a very long time for twenty-two people to be locked together in a relatively small space. Some of the squad spent time playing a low-gravity game, something like badminton. Schiff had found a tennis ball, of all things, on Washington, and he and Castillo started batting it back and forth across the freezer bay in long, slow, precise arcs. Eventually, the rules for a game were developed, others joined in, and Carlson ended up refereeing a loudly contested tournament. Carlson didn't let the tournament interfere with our chores around the ship, and Francesca and Robert didn't interfere with the game.

The ship's trajectory to Antarctica took us in through the middle of the system, between Iota and Asia. Using the pull of both the stars saved us fuel and gave us a chance to study Asia itself more closely. Francesca sent three probes to orbit around Asia to take a variety of readings. She also sent one to check out Iota, though there was far less mystery surrounding it. The Iota probe did find the shattered remains of the colonists' original beam assembly. That discovery sparked a lot of conversation, and Gallo made a startling admission:

"I never understood how a beam works."

Brady responded. "You don't? Look. It's simple." She called over to another soldier on the far side of the bay. "Townsend. Throw me the ball." Private Townsend tossed the tennis ball across the bay to Brady. Then she threw it to Gallo.

"That ball had information on it. How long did it take to get to you?"

"About a second."

"If I said to you, 'Gallo, you're a waste of space,' how long would that information take to get to you?"

"A lot less time, since it's traveling at the speed of sound."

"Very good. And if I did this—" She winked at him. He grinned back. I found myself frowning. "—what about that information?"

"Speed of light. No time at all."

"No, it took time. Just a very small amount of time, since you're so close. Now, let's see..." Brady started looking through the stuff under her cot. She pulled out her mag rifle and removed the barrel. It was a slim metal tube about half a meter long. She pointed the barrel at Gallo's chest, just touching him with it. Gallo was grinning like this was some sort of foreplay. Brady smiled, then whacked her end of the barrel as hard as she could, pushing it into Gallo.

"Hey!" he protested.

"How long did *that* information take to get to you?"

"What did I do?" he asked.

"Come on. How long?"

"Almost no time."

"Right. But if the barrel were perfectly rigid and didn't weigh anything at all... it wouldn't take *any* time. Zero. Neutrinos have no mass. There's a dozen or so lasers directing a concentrated beam of neutrinos across light years of space." Brady gave the barrel another shove. "When I push from this end, you get the information immediately. And when you push from your end—" Gallo grabbed his end of the barrel and shoved Brady back roughly. She took the abuse with a smile. "—then I get the information just as fast. All we have to do is make the entire beam vibrate, and the vibrations are the signals; we can communicate instantaneously, from one star to another, as long as we have a beam in place between them."

"Uh-huh." Gallo seemed less interested in Brady's explanation than he did in his bruised chest. He walked off. I watched as Brady reassembled her mag rifle.

"I thought you had a pill." Francesca had snuck up behind me.

"What?"

"To control your sexual urges. You soldiers take pills."

"It's a time release hormonal suppressant." The implants, usually referred to as monk-boxes by the troops, aren't a secret, but they aren't advertised by the ECAF, either. A subtle chemical cocktail is continuously introduced into the soldier's bloodstream to turn off the natural sexual instinct. For centuries it was thought that the drive of sexual conquest was tied to the drive of military conquest, but research showed otherwise, and what would have otherwise been a distraction was removed from the equation of our lives in the service. "It's a little more complex than just pills."

"Still, it doesn't seem to work."

"You mean Gallo? He's harmless. He's just a little boy

yanking on Brady's pigtails."

"I don't mean Gallo." Francesca was grinning at me.

"Brady?" I asked. "I don't see that at all."

"Captain, I'm talking about you."

"Me?"

"I see the way you look at her."

"She's a soldier under my command," I said, stone faced. Francesca grinned playfully.

"You don't look that way at Private James."

"James? She's been in the Force for five years. Brady's green. She needs more instruction."

"Whatever you say." Francesca walked back to the bridge, her disbelief hanging in the air like a bad smell.

Did I have some sort of feelings for Brady? I didn't think so. She was fifteen years younger than me, for one thing. And for another, she *was* a soldier under my command. Men and women had served side by side since fifty years before we were frozen for this trip. Various military structures had farted around for centuries, trying to give women a place in the fighting forces, but they shoehorned them in with quotas and special rules. Now, there is one standard for any branch of the Force. Every trooper under me can run the same distance and carry the same weight, and that's why out of nineteen of them, there are only four women. Look in any submarine back on Earth, or the pilot training program around Jupiter, and you'll see far more women than men. Everyone finds their level.

The monk-boxes made the whole transition smoother, and they became a part of the culture of the ECAF. And that was why I didn't have a *crush* on one of the members of my squad. I decided to go explain that to that cheeky android.

I walked onto the bridge so fast Robert couldn't turn off the projector before I saw what he was working on.

"What was that?" I asked, advancing on him.

"I don't know what you mean." Robert was a good pilot, but a bad liar. I grabbed him by the collar and pulled him out of the chair. "Stop it!" I punched up a redo function and brought his visual simulation back to life. Rotating in front of us was a schematic of a seven-sided piece of metal, covered in a cross-hatch pattern, bent into a distinctive shape, a cross between a serving dish and an orchid...

I turned on him. He was a good ten centimeters taller than me, but my mood made it clear who was in charge.

"I don't know what you think you're doing—"

"Research." He actually had the balls to interrupt me. I was amazed.

"You are researching something that you have been told to *leave alone!*"

Francesca came onto the bridge, with a couple of privates following. I quickly hit a button to delete the holo image.

"You can't stop me from thinking!" Robert was filled with some sort of scientific fervor that I couldn't and still don't understand.

"You didn't come up with that design out of the circuits in your head," I said, reverting to android abuse. It was ugly, but I wanted to hammer this point home. "You stole that description from *my personal log!*"

Three more troops entered the bridge, drawn by the raised voices. One was Brady. I didn't look at her.

"Captain, I—"

"Robert, there is no more discussion on this point! You have broken ECAF security, and you will be dealt with severely when we return to Earth. Until that time, my troops will conduct daily searches of all ship's systems for any more references to the gravity mirror, and if any more are found, you will be placed under arrest for the duration of this mission. Is that understood?"

Silence. Robert looked to Francesca for support, but her look back to him was absent any fervor. She seemed disappointed. Robert, broken, replied: "Yes, sir."

I ordered Brady to delete the simulation, and I stormed off the bridge and went to my tent in the freezing bay. I collapsed on my cot, hoping my performance was believable enough to convince everyone in that room that what Robert had built in the computer's simulation was an accurate representation of the gravity mirror. I didn't want anyone other than Brady to know what it really looked like. I certainly wouldn't have written anything close to an accurate description in my service log. Or in this journal, either.

✿✿

Three days out from Antarctica, we ran across an iceberg in space.

The object was roughly spherical, about a kilometer in diameter, and almost pure water. A handful of small thrusters dotted its surface. The Iota System was starved for water, except on Antarctica, the planet farthest out from the star. Using ships to transport the water was impractical to say the least, so the Antarcticans devised this method of transport. They melted water on the surface and drew it up into space with huge, counterweighted siphons, basically straws that hung from orbit, not unlike the space elevators back on Mars and Earth. They froze out the water into huge balls of ice in orbit, and then flung them in towards whichever planet had purchased the water. The thrusters allowed for minor orbit corrections, but more importantly, since the trips lasted years, sometimes decades, the thrusters also allowed for a guarantee: if the Antarcticans didn't get paid, they could stop the iceberg mid-transit and redirect it to another customer, or simply put it into orbit around Iota, wherever it happened to be. And since only they knew the berg's exact location, it would be almost impossible for anyone else to retrieve it.

We ran across this one easily, so we had to assume that the Antarcticans had, at some point after the war began, stopped all shipments of water, leaving behind dozens, maybe hundreds of these man-made comets roaming the system. This was a drastic step they had taken. If anyone had been left alive in-system, they might have come out to the distant planet for water—and revenge.

It was difficult to decide if this was good or bad news for our rescue mission.

Faster-than-light beam communications were necessary from system to system, but within a system, radio was still the preferred mode. Throughout the first half of the trip from Earth on *Telperion*, Robert and Francesca had received a myriad of extremely faint radio signals from all the planets of Iota, but there were none after the ignition of Asia. We continued to monitor as we toured the wrecked system, but we heard nothing.

As we made our way into Antarctic orbit, we still hoped that the survivors would send us some message, so faint that it was indistinguishable from background radiation until we were this close. Still, all we heard was silence. There were small settlements near the ice fields, but the planet's only main city was in the highlands, a place called Amundsen. Robert brought *Telperion* into orbit, and we prepared our last excursion. I left Privates Scott and Malone on the colony ship as backup and to keep the androids in line, if it came to that. Everyone else went down to the planet.

It was becoming repetitious. Another shuttle trip to another dark, lifeless dome. We swept the dome with practiced efficiency, but this time, we found no bodies. There was no carefully constructed tomb, no chaotic scenes of destruction. Here, in the city of Amundsen, there was just nothing. I called back up to the colony ship and asked Francesca to search the area around the dome for any sign of inhabitation. She found evidence of a crash site to the south, near a round, shallow basin. There were also signs of construction in the basin. The basin was three kilometers away. We had a march ahead of us.

We saw the tracks soon enough. Heavy vehicles, earth-moving equipment probably, had made this journey before us. Antarctica was devoid of any atmosphere, so these tracks could have been made five days earlier, or five decades. At least we knew we were hiking in the right direction.

There was very little chatter from the troops over the radio. It was daytime, but the dim light from Iota only lit the planet a little less efficiently than the Moon does Earth. It felt like nighttime, which put us into a somber mood.

And we were all tired of searching for survivors that just weren't there. So we expected disappointment when Sharples said, "Look."

We topped a rise, and down on the plain below we saw what the construction equipment was for: ten thousand graves filled the basin, all in neat rows, the mounds of dark brown dirt unmistakable in the dim light. Most of us, myself included, stopped, overwhelmed by the misery that we were witness to, not only today, but throughout this mission. If I had let myself, I might have stood there and cried.

"So," Brady said, "who buried them?"

Just then I wondered if Francesca was right, because I could've kissed Brady. "You're right," I said. "There could still be survivors. Fan out, look for shelters. There might be caves or tunnels. Tate, Schiff, go check that crashed ship. The rest of us will stay in the basin for now." There was little excitement in the soldiers' footsteps, but at least they had some task. I continued down the makeshift road into the cemetery. The first grave I came across was about two meters long. I knelt down to pay my respects. At one end of the mound, I saw a small white stick in the ground. I picked it out of the dirt. It was a memory stick.

"Who has a media player?" I asked on the open frequency.

"Right here," Gallo said, who I saw was already running toward me. I gave him the memory stick and he inserted it into his player. "It's just text, sir, and not very much."

"Read it."

"'Jennifer Alexis Cooper, daughter of Mary and Angelo Cooper. Age 13.' That's it."

"A headstone." I took the memory stick back and replaced it at the head of the grave.

"Captain?" It was Silverberg. "I've got something here. I think it's a tunnel." Silverberg was waving from the east side of the basin. We all ran over there. The ground was smoothed out and ran like a ramp into the side of the basin, where a tunnel had been cut. The slope was shallow. The ramp, which was only a few meters wide, ran almost half a kilometer before it hit the tunnel. There seemed to be no door, and it was dark inside.

I assigned four troops to stay in the cemetery. I led the rest down the ramp. We approached with caution, but there was still no sign of life. At the mouth of the tunnel, I split another group of four off to guard the entrance. The other ten of us entered the cave.

Low light goggles did no good after only a few steps, so we switched to infrared. The temperature variations in the rock walls were slight, but enough for us to make out the features of the cave. It continued at the same slight angle and at the same width for as far as we could see. Once again, it was Sharples that saw something ahead.

"Right there. A hundred meters up. On the left."

"I don't see it," Gallo said.

"It's black."

"Everything is black," Brady said.

"It's blacker."

I turned up the gain on my infrared and I saw it. A shape, difficult to make out, that looked like a hole in the cavern walls, which were otherwise quite regular. If it was that black with infravision, it must have been *colder* than the rock. As I squinted at the ungainly shape, it brought to mind a table... and then it moved.

"Did you see that?" Brady asked.

"Everyone stay calm," I said. One of the legs of the table shifted, threatening to topple it over.

"Should we turn on a light, Captain?" Gallo asked.

"Negative."

Another leg of the thing moved. I was concerned that we were making contact with some indigenous life form that might react badly to a stab of light. I edged closer. The thing was definitely aware of us, trying to come to us, but very slowly, almost as if it were in pain.

"I don't like this," Gallo said.

"Shut up," Brady said.

I kept moving forward, trying to get a better look at the thing. Then I heard something over my radio that froze me. It was almost a voice, but distorted, stuttering like a lagging data stream.

"Jo-o-o-o-o-o-o-o-o-o-o-o-o-o-o—"

"Who did that?" I asked. Silence from the others. They hadn't done it. And they must have heard it, too. It was on the common band.

"Jo-o-o-o-o-o-o-o-o-n-a-a-a-a-a-a-a-a—"

Now my blood was frozen along with the rest of me. This creature was calling my name. It moved again, faster this time, a leg in front and a leg in back dragging the rest of the shambling creature forward.

"Lex-lex-lex-lex-lex-lex-lex—"

My last name, or part of it. I took a step back, but I couldn't take my eyes of the thing.

"Captain?" It was Gallo again. "What's going on?"

"Light, Gallo. Now!"

Gallo turned on a lamp and filled the cavern with harsh light. The creature shuddered and stumbled under the light, but still seemed to be made of shadow.

"Oh, my God!" Brady said, and she ran up to the creature. I almost cried out to make her stop. She didn't know what she was doing. It was going to attack.

She gently laid the thing on its side. "Captain, we need to get him back to the shuttle!"

I didn't understand. I stood there like a statue. "Captain, switch to visible light," she said. I hadn't turned of the infravision, which was why the creature had stayed black. I switched over to regular light mode and saw Brady cradling an unsuited man in her arms. I ran up to them, past the others who were crowding in.

It was a man, but alive in the bitter cold, with nothing to breathe. I realized he must have been an android. He was conscious, aware of us, but unable to move properly. Only his right arm and his left leg seemed to function at all. He must have spoken to us with a radio implant. But I didn't understand who it was until Gallo said, "Hey, I know him."

I looked at the face more closely. He appeared to be thirty years old, with brown hair and eyes. Even a few freckles.

"Your name is Clark," I said. The android nodded

spastically.

We carried Clark to the shuttle and immediately turned up the heat in the cabin. Androids run on ambient heat, so it was no wonder he was almost dead. When his ability to speak returned, the first thing he said was, "Lois. Cave." I sent three troops back into the cave to find his copilot. They brought her to the shuttle, another nondescript brunette thirty-year-old, but unlike Clark, she was unconscious.

"Heat," Clark said. I nodded and Grant increased the temperature in the cabin as high as it would go.

"We're taking you to our ship," I said.

&#9672;&#9672;

Back on *Telperion*, Robert and Francesca went to work trying to revive Lois in their stateroom. When it was clear they would have to perform some sort of surgery, they asked Clark to leave. I shouldered him up off the edge of the bed and guided him out to the bridge, to the command chair. Even after it closed, his eyes remained fixed on that door.

"Clark?" I asked.

"Yes," he said, unmoving.

"Are you up to answering a few questions?"

"Ask."

There were ten others in the room, hovering, watching. I made a gesture to Carlson, and she herded everyone off the bridge.

"How long have you been on Antarctica?"

"Since the war," he said. "You know about the war?"

"Some." I gave him our sketch of what we thought had gone on sixty years earlier. He nodded.

"That's about right."

"Were you attacked?"

"No. We thought we might be, but we were lucky."

I had a flash of the cemetery, and shuddered. Lucky. Clark was still watching the closed door. I put a hand on his shoulder, noting that he really felt quite cool. He turned to me.

"They'll do what they can," I said.

He nodded. "I know. But I've been with her for so long; I don't think I can live without her." He paused, then laughed. A real laugh. "I'll bet you think I'm just being dramatic."

"I know a little about your lives."

"We've been together for two hundred forty years. That's Earth years. Do you think that's strange, that I still think in Earth years?"

"No. Not at all."

"Lois always tried to make me convert things into Europe years like everyone else around Iota. I was just stubborn about it." He paused again, his eyes quivering, about to cry. He shook his head and stopped himself. I marveled at the human simulation that I was watching. And it was all real to him. He was really feeling these things.

"You've been through a lot."

"That's an understatement," he said, and he laughed again.

"We saw the graves."

Clark tilted his head. I thought it might be a malfunction, but he was just confused. "Graves?"

"Down on the planet... In the basin..."

"Oh, those aren't graves," he said.

"They aren't—" The door opened and Clark jumped up. Francesca came out.

"How is she?" Clark asked.

"She's got a ways to go, but I think she'll be alright." Francesca's smile was like the sun. Clark let himself cry now, and gave her a hug. "Go on in. She's awake."

"Thank you."

Clark ran into the stateroom. Through the doorway I watched their reunion, until Francesca closed the door and gave me a scolding look.

✪✪

Lois and Clark told the story in tandem, not really finishing each other's sentences, but alternating thought by thought. The two pilots, the original team that brought *Hermione* to Iota with the first colonists, had been present at a celebration commemorating that event when the war began right in front of them. They didn't waste any time. As soon as courtesy allowed, they shuttled up to their old ship, which was orbiting Gandhi, one of the Asian moons, as part of the anniversary. They were ostensibly to park it in orbit around the gas giant as it always had been.

Instead, they fled to Antarctica. *Hermione*, low on fuel from the early days of transporting settlers around the system and her recent demonstration in the skies of Gandhi, couldn't make for the distant icy planet very fast. She was still weeks away from Antarctica when Asia exploded. The ship was damaged by the leading edge of the blast. They couldn't maneuver into an orbit, but they managed to crash land her near Amundsen.

With the rest of the Iota System totally destroyed, the sixteen thousand Antarcticans—and their two new immigrants—had a hard road ahead of them. There would be no more food shipments from Europe, no more electronics from Asia, and most importantly, no uranium from Australia. The pervasive rumor that Antarctica had an abundant supply of hoarded deuterium and tritium was just that: a rumor. They were as dependent on fission as any planet, and more so than some. They didn't have any geothermal possibilities, and solar power was little more than a dream that far away from Iota.

So the rationing began. It was difficult, but everyone accepted that their lot in life had changed, and changed drastically. Time spent writing or building or composing was now entirely devoted to survival. Everyone was pressed into service, tending machines and crops alike, using human labor to save power for the heaters. People tried to be optimistic, but no matter how they crunched the numbers, there wasn't enough energy to sustain the population until help was scheduled to arrive, help in the form of a colony resupply ship called *Telperion*.

It was the Governor of Antarctica, a woman named Cecilia Matson, who came up with a solution, a way to give the thousands of survivors a chance. The answer was lying in pieces, three kilometers south of the dome, a ship built with one purpose: to sustain human life in suspended animation for decades. Those mounds in the basin weren't graves. Under each mound was a transplanted freezing chamber, carried from the crash site. One by one, the Antarcticans took their places in the chambers. It was quite a production, requiring a pressure tent for the occupant and a power pack to initiate the freezing process safely. The chambers couldn't remain powered, but the temperature on the planet, at least at night, was low enough to maintain stasis. Even the feeble light of Iota might warm the chamber too much, so each one was buried under a blanket of protective soil.

Freezing everyone on the planet took half a European year. Matson herself insisted on being the last, and when she was asleep, only Clark and Lois remained, rationing the remaining precious energy that would generate the heat that they needed, playing against time, waiting for rescue.

✺✺

Carlson worked it out. It would take ten weeks to move all the freezing chambers on the planet up to *Telperion* and get them installed. No one minded extending the stay around Iota, not with this kind of task to keep them busy. Even Gallo seemed to be humbled by the concept of having saved the lives of 16,423 people—and two androids.

As we readied our next trip to the surface, I noticed the four androids in some sort of deep conference in Robert and Francesca's stateroom. For half a second I wondered if they were communicating digitally, but they were just whispering. I didn't want to listen in, but I had business on the bridge with the computer. A few words rose above the muttering, but nothing I could understand. Apparently, some decision had been made, and they were all happy as they walked out of the room toward me. Three of them filed off to help with some task, but Robert came up to me.

"What was that all about?" I asked.

"We were working out the living arrangements for the trip back to Earth."

"Oh." I wasn't sure why that was so difficult. Must have been an android thing.

"Clark and Lois were worried about... boredom."

"Boredom?" I laughed. "They just spent how many decades alone on a practically lifeless planet? At least they'll have you and Francesca for company now."

The look Robert gave me was piercing. He seemed truly amazed by what I had said. "That's what I told them."

He turned to leave, then turned back.

"One other thing, Captain?"

"Yes?"

He paused. He seemed to be searching for the right words.

"I've thought more about your position on the... research. It is possible you weren't mistaken."

I suppressed a laugh. After everything we had seen, all the tragedy and destruction and death, it took two sick androids to bring it home to him. I suppose he really was human after all.

"Robert, I just want you to know, I am very glad you'll be driving me home."

# Notes on Iota Horologii

The star known as Iota Horologii (HD 17051) is just visible to the naked eye in the skies of the Southern Hemisphere of Earth. It is located in the constellation Horologium (The Clock), which was introduced by Nicolas Louis de Lacaille. His catalogue of the southern sky, *Coelum Australe Stelliferum*, was published posthumously in 1763.

The star gained some notoriety in 1999 when it became one of the first several dozen stars beyond Earth's home system discovered to have an orbiting planet. The members of the team that made the discovery of the gas giant were Martin Kürster, Michael Endl, Sebastian Els, Artie P. Hatzes, William D. Cochran, Stefan Döbereiner and Konrad Dennerl. They named the planet Iota Horologii b.

A second wave of planetary discoveries—of terrestrial worlds—included findings pointing to at least three rocky planets around Iota Horologii, tentatively named Iota Horologii c, d and e. These discoveries were made simultaneously by Ester Arroway and Fung Cho in 2034.

Verification of the existence of these four planets—and the discovery of two others—was made in transit to Iota Horologii by Lois and Clark on *Hermione* during the years of 2215-18.

For details of the bodies in the Iota system, reference the chart on the following page.

| Body | Diameter (km) | Mass (kg) | Gravity (g)* | Distance (AU) | Revolutionary Period (days)* | Period (hrs)* |
|---|---|---|---|---|---|---|
| **Iota** | **1,405,000** | **2.05E+30** | - | - | - | - |
| **Australia** | **4,503** | **2.63E+23** | **0.35** | **0.35** | **75** | **1789** |
| **Asia** | **187,634** | **4.29E+27** | - | **0.93** | **322** | **8** |
| Ghandi | 6,483 | 7.84E+23 | 0.51 | 0.015 | 14 | 347 |
| Ganges | 2,064 | 2.53E+22 | 0.16 | 0.00030 | 3 | 71 |
| Azuka | 5,714 | 5.37E+23 | 0.45 | 0.022 | 26 | 617 |
| Fuji | 1,533 | 1.04E+22 | 0.12 | 0.00032 | 4 | 96 |
| **Europe** | **9,989** | **2.87E+24** | **0.78** | **1.22** | **483** | **25** |
| DeGaulle | 2,751 | 5.99E+22 | 0.22 | 0.0025 | 38 | 903 |
| Capra | 1,545 | 1.06E+22 | 0.12 | 0.0077 | 205 | 4924 |
| **Africa** | **8,884** | **2.02E+24** | **0.70** | **1.70** | **798** | **20** |
| **America** | **15,060** | **9.83E+24** | **1.18** | **3.90** | **2772** | **18** |
| Washington | 3,019 | 7.92E+22 | 0.24 | 0.0050 | 58 | 1389 |
| **Antarctica** | **3,702** | **1.46E+23** | **0.29** | **27** | **50775** | **47** |
| **Sun** | **1,392,000** | **1.99E+30** | - | - | - | - |
| **Earth** | **12,756** | **5.97E+24** | **1.00** | **1.00** | **365** | **24** |
| Moon | 3,476 | 7.35E+22 | 0.17 | 0.0026 | 27 | 655 |
| **Mars** | **6,974** | **6.42E+23** | **0.38** | **1.52** | **687** | **25** |
| **Jupiter** | **142,984** | **1.90E+37** | - | **5.20** | **4329** | **10** |

*All measures based on Earth Standard

# Notes on Iotan Calendar

The Iotan Calendar, adopted by all the planets and moons of Iota Horologii, was based on the European year, which lasts 463.5 European days. Each year began on the anniversary of the first manned European landing and was divided into twelve months—as in the Earth calendar—with each month containing 38 or 39 days, as follows:

| | |
|---|---|
| January | 39 |
| February | 38/39 |
| March | 39 |
| April | 38 |
| May | 39 |
| June | 38 |
| July | 39 |
| August | 39 |
| September | 38 |
| October | 39 |
| November | 38 |
| December | 39 |

To account for the extra half-day in each European year, a Leap Day was added to February in even numbered years, much like the quadrennial Leap Day in the Earth calendar. This extra day was also known locally on Europe as Calm Day, referring to the planet's relatively stable weather patterns during even numbered years.

Observance of holidays around Iota tended to follow patterns from Earth culture: e.g. Christmas was celebrated on December 25. The traditional calculation of Easter, with its dependence on lunar cycles, was abandoned early on. Christian Iotans chose to celebrate Easter on the last Sunday of April.

Since the length of a European day was slightly longer than an Earth day (25.02 hours, compared to Earth's 23.93 hours), the calendars of the two planets were not in sync on a day-to-day basis. This caused little or no confusion for native Iotans, since they maintained only the barest contact with Earth after the initial colonization was complete.

Variations in day or year length on the inhabited moons and planets of the Iota System caused special problems for some citizens. The settlers on Australia and Antarctica lived in perpetual darkness; their domes were programmed to follow European rhythms. The peoples of America, Africa and the moons of Asia contended with a calendar that did not conform to local patterns of Iota's rising and setting. Dozens of ad-hoc calendar/timing systems went in and out of fashion, but for official record keeping, the Iotan Calendar remained the standard through the eighty-year history of the colony.

# Timeline

| Iotan Calendar | | Earth Calendar |
|---|---|---|
| December 8, 58 B.L. | *Hermione* launches from Earth. | *December 5, 2182* |
| November 26, 1 B.L. | *Hermione* arrives in Iota System. | *March 11, 2258* |
| January 1, 1 | First landing on Europe | *May 4, 2258* |
| January 1, 76 | Secession of Europe, America and Antarctica | *June 25, 2357* |
| August 28, 76 | *Telperion* launches from Earth | *May 1, 2358* |
| April 15, 80 | Destruction of Iotan beam assembly | *February 22, 2363* |
| September 8, 80 | Africa destroyed | *September 3, 2363* |
| November 30, 80 | America destroyed; Asia ignited | *December 15, 2363* |
| July 1, 125 | *Telperion* arrives in Iota System | *November 30, 2422* |

# About the Author

Russell Lutz makes his novel publishing debut with *Iota Cycle*. Holding two degrees in mathematics and after a decade of experience in retail supply chain management, he is uniquely qualified to write speculative fiction. His short stories have previously appeared in several webzines and magazines, including Byzarium, The SiNK, scifantastic, and anotherealm. He won the 2005 SFFWorld First Place prize for short fiction for the *Iota Cycle* story "Fall." His story "Athens 3004" appeared in the short fiction anthology *Silverthought: Ignition*. His current projects include a follow up to *Iota Cycle*. He lives, works, reads, writes, watches movies and ponders the imponderable in Seattle.

LaVergne, TN USA
04 February 2010
172164LV00002B/1/A